"What plans do you have?"

No one had ever asked her that in her life, and indeed, she hadn't thought about it herself. "I...um...why, to see my son grow to be a fine young knight, and to make the best ale I can," Mair stammered.

Very gently Trystan reached out and took her shoulders in his strong hands. "Is that all?" he asked softly as he pulled her into his embrace, another emotion smoldering in his gray eyes.

"Take your hands off me, Trystan," she whispered.

In a way, he did, for his hold loosened. Nevertheless, his breathing quickened, matching the rapid rhythm of her own.

Then he slowly moved his hands down her arms in a gesture that was more like a caress than anything else. "Order me to go, Mair, and I will."

As his fingers began another slow, tantalizing journey, Mair *couldn't* ask him to leave....

Dear Reader,

In *The Bonny Bride* by award-winning author Deborah Hale, a poor young woman sets sail for Nova Scotia from England as a mail-order bride to a wealthy man, yet meets her true soul mate on board the ship. Will she choose love or money? Margaret Moore, who also writes mainstream historicals for Avon Books, returns with *A Warrior's Kiss,* a passionate marriage-of-convenience story and the next in her ongoing medieval WARRIOR series. Theresa Michaels's new Western, *Once a Hero,* is a gripping and emotion-filled story about a cowboy who rescues a female fugitive and unexpectedly falls in love with her as they go in search of a lost treasure. For readers who enjoy discovering new writers, *The Virgin Spring* by Golden Heart winner Debra Lee Brown is for you. Here, a Scottish laird finds an amnesiac woman beside a spring and must resist his desire for her, as he believes she is forbidden to him.

For the next two months we are going to be asking readers to let us know what you are looking for from Harlequin Historicals. We hope you'll participate by sending your ideas to us at:

Harlequin Historicals
300 E. 42nd St.
New York, NY 10017

Q. What do you like about Harlequin Historicals?

_____

_____

Q. What *don't* you like about Harlequin Historicals?

_____

_____

Whatever your tastes in reading, you'll be sure to find a romantic journey back to the past between the covers of a Harlequin Historicals novel. We hope you'll join us next month, too!

Sincerely,

Tracy Farrell,
Senior Editor

Margaret Moore

A Warrior's Kiss

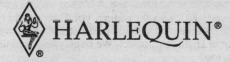

HARLEQUIN®

TORONTO • NEW YORK • LONDON
AMSTERDAM • PARIS • SYDNEY • HAMBURG
STOCKHOLM • ATHENS • TOKYO • MILAN • MADRID
PRAGUE • WARSAW • BUDAPEST • AUCKLAND

ISBN 0-373-29104-3

A WARRIOR'S KISS

Copyright © 2000 by Margaret Wilkins

Visit us at www.romance.net

Printed in U.S.A.

Please address questions and book requests to:
Harlequin Reader Service
U.S.: 3010 Walden Ave., P.O. Box 1325, Buffalo, NY 14269
Canadian: P.O. Box 609, Fort Erie, Ont. L2A 5X3

Chapter One

Pleased to have a moment's respite from the noisy celebrations going on in the hall below, Sir Trystan DeLanyea strolled along the upper wall walk of his father's castle.

The harvest had been a good one, and all who lived in or near the castle of Craig Fawr were feasting and playing and dancing in the great hall. By this time in the evening, the air was thick with the scents of smoke, tallow and sweating bodies mingling with expensive perfumes and spices.

Taking a deep breath of the cool, refreshing air, Trystan sighed and leaned against the inner curtain wall's merlon. His father had spent years building this fortress after his return from the Crusade. Now it was as strong and comfortable as any lord could wish for, as well as an imposing tribute to his father's determination and trading acumen.

As Trystan let his gaze rove over the inner ward,

he spotted the place where, three years ago, he had
finally hit a perfect bull's-eye with his lance, something not even Griffydd, his elder brother, had ever
been able to do. That had been a great day—until
that impertinent wench Mair had happened by with
a cartload of ale and ruined his delight by observ-
ing that the targets seemed to be getting larger
every time she came to the castle.

Although he was the Baron DeLanyea's son, she
had never respected him, or even liked him. She
had always teased him and made sport of him,
from the days they were children.

He didn't doubt it would have been different if
he were the eldest, like Griffydd, or a baron in his
own right, like his cousin and foster brother,
Dylan.

But he wasn't. To all and sundry around Craig
Fawr, Trystan was still looked on as a "boy," as
Dylan persisted in addressing him, even though he
had earned his knighthood.

Someday, though, that was going to change,
Trystan silently vowed. He, Sir Trystan DeLanyea,
was going to become the most famous, wealthy
and respected DeLanyea of all, more so even than
his father, who had lost an eye fighting with King
Richard in the Holy Land.

Trystan permitted himself a small smile as he
considered again the very pleasant way he had realized he could start his journey on the road to

fame and success: he would marry the proper wife, and who better than the most beautiful and desirable Norman noblewoman he had ever met, Lady Rosamunde D'Heureux, who was visiting here with her father?

Although Sir Edward D'Heureux did not boast a great title, his family had far more power and influence within the court than many, including Trystan's own. Any man allied with him would have tremendous opportunities for advancement. Indeed, the man who could win Lady Rosamunde's hand could surely expect notice from the king himself. And a man who had the notice of the king could go very far indeed, certainly farther than an older brother already married to a woman from the north, or a cousin ensconced in his Welsh castle.

The chance of such a marriage didn't seem at all impossible as Trystan recalled how Lady Rosamunde had smiled and danced with him in her demure, ladylike way before she had retired for the evening.

He should retire, too, he thought as he stifled a yawn. He should be waiting to escort Lady Rosamunde to the chapel for mass in the morning.

He turned and headed back toward the stairs leading to the inner courtyard. He passed the sentry on duty near the first watchtower and, barely noticing the guard's brisk salute, continued around the tower and entered a more secluded part of the wall walk. The rays of moonlight did not penetrate this dim corner of the walk.

Suddenly, two hands reached out and grabbed his woolen tunic, yanking him backward into the darkest part of the shadow. Before he could call out, the person attacking him pressed her voluptuous body against his and kissed him passionately.

It was a kiss such as a man might dream of. The perfect kiss, firm and yet soft, lips moving with hot, fervent desire, taking his very breath away. Her mouth tasted of honey and spices, like mead, and wisps of hair tickled his cheek.

A man could well get drunk on such a kiss.

As his own ardor increased and his embrace tightened about her shapely form, Trystan wondered who it was.

Lady Rosamunde? She was too timid and delicate for this earthy passion, and she would taste of wine.

One of the serving wenches? Aye, perhaps, if there was one so bold.

Did it matter?

The heady scent of mead seemed to mingle with the night air and become a part of it, and him, as he gave himself up to the enjoyment of this unexpectedly passionate moment.

Then, as suddenly as the kiss began, the woman broke it and shoved him away. "You're not Ivor!"

she cried in an angry whisper and an all-too-familiar voice.

A curse flew from Trystan's lips, in no small part because he should have known who would taste and smell of mead.

"By God's holy heart, Mair!" he declared in a whisper just as angry as he grabbed her slender shoulders. "What in the name of the saints are you doing?"

He couldn't see the young, unmarried woman who brewed ale and mead for her living very well, but he knew she had been at the feast. How could he miss her, in her best gown of scarlet silk trimmed with green and gold, as fine as any high-born lady's garment? A well-fitted gown it was, too, no doubt designed to show off her shapely form and attract male attention. Round her head she wore a circlet of scarlet ribbon that streamed out behind her like a knight's pennant as she danced.

Aye, Mair had been everywhere at the feast, it had seemed, dancing and smiling and laughing and tossing her rich, chestnut mane of hair about like some kind of demented, blithe spirit of festivity, flirting with all the men—except for him, because she knew better.

"As even you might guess, I am waiting for Ivor," she retorted, as mocking and bold and shameless as always.

"The captain of the guard?" Trystan demanded, thinking of the dark-haired, muscular fellow his father had recently promoted to that position.

"Not that it's any of your business," Mair replied as, with a disdainful sniff, she went to push past him.

Hearing the sound of approaching footsteps, Trystan shoved her back into the corner and blockaded her there with his body.

"What do you—?" she protested.

"Be quiet! The last thing I want is for anybody to see us together," he growled quietly.

She laughed softly, the mischievous sound so low, he knew only he would hear it. "Oh, we mustn't have that, must we, or Angharad will be thinking her prediction is about to come true."

The guard made his turn and started back toward his post, something Trystan only half-noted, just as he only partly paid attention to Mair's reminder that Angharad, credited with the Sight, had ridiculously prophesied that one day he and this impertinent alewife would be married.

The greater part of his mind was desperately trying to ignore the sensation of his body against Mair's, and the memory of that kiss. "You and I both know Angharad is dead wrong about that," he muttered. "I would never marry you."

"What's the matter, Sir Trystan?" Mair inquired in a teasing whisper. "You sound all out of breath."

"Nothing is the matter with me." To prove that, he moved even closer. "Where's Arthur?" he demanded, naming the illegitimate child she had borne ten years before. "He can't be with his father, for Dylan is not here tonight."

"No, nor Dylan's wife, either. How sad for you."

Instantly Trystan's jaw clenched. "Whatever I once felt for Genevieve is gone. Can you say the same of Dylan?"

Mair quietly laughed, the sound a throaty bubble of mirth full of genuine good humor. It was the same reaction she always had when he tried to speak with her, as if serious matters were immaterial if *he* spoke of them. "Jealous, are you?"

"Never of you and him."

"Ah, well, considering Dylan hasn't been with me since before Arthur first saw the light of day, I suppose I should commend you on your wisdom."

"I said, *never* of you and him," he growled.

She bowed her head with mocking acceptance. "Very well, I believe you. And since you are kind enough to inquire, my son is with Trefor and Angharad tonight," she replied, naming Dylan's other bastard son, and his mother.

"At least Angharad knows how to behave."

"Angharad won't take another lover because she's too arrogant. After having a baron's child, she won't love any man who isn't noble."

"Did she tell you that?"

"You know Angharad. Do you doubt it?"

"Perhaps she regrets bearing Dylan's child."

Mair laughed again. "Don't be daft. She doesn't, and neither do I. Or is that the Norman influence talking? You know the Welsh don't care about that. We're too sensible."

"That is not the word I would use."

"What word would you use? No, wait, let me guess," she answered, putting her slender finger against his lips. "Sinful." She slowly dragged her finger down his chin. "Lustful. Lascivious."

Feeling aroused in spite of his determination not to be, he batted her hand away. "Aren't you the least bit ashamed about having a child out of wedlock?"

"*Anwyl,* now I know you've been too long among the Normans! No, of course I'm not."

"And it doesn't bother you that Dylan married somebody else?"

"Why should it? We never spoke of marriage. Besides, we were finished long before he met Genevieve."

"I will never, ever, understand you."

"Maybe I don't want you to."

"And I don't care what you do, or who you do

it with," he retorted, nearly overwhelmed with the desire to taste her sweet, spicy lips again, to hold her vibrant, womanly body against his.

"Good, is that."

"Stay here, then, and meet your lover."

"I think I had better go find him, for he is late. Now let me pass."

"I am not stopping you."

"You're in my way."

The sound of his heartbeat throbbed in his ears. "Am I?"

"Yes."

He didn't move away. Instead he gave in to the temptation he could no longer fight and pulled her into his arms.

Then he kissed her with all the fierce, unbridled passion unleashed by the first touch of her lips upon his.

She seemed to yield—but only for a moment, before she pushed him away.

"I don't even like you!" Mair protested, meaning it, believing it, in spite of the incredible feelings of desire and longing Trystan DeLanyea's kiss aroused.

No, she didn't like Trystan, with his cool gray eyes that always seemed to find fault with her, as if condemning her for enjoying all that life had to offer, and all that men did, too. To be sure, he was handsome, like all the DeLanyeas, with his cousin's dark, curling hair and sensual lips. He dressed well, too, his black tunic and breeches showing off the muscles that only hours of training and riding could produce.

But there were other men as handsome as he, and plenty with more of a sense of humor. Indeed, if he had Dylan's best features, he also had the grave, gray eyes of his elder brother, the stern and forbidding Griffydd DeLanyea, who wore his honor like armor.

"I don't like you, either," he replied.

"Then get out of my way."

He half turned, making a grand gesture of invitation to walk past him. She took a step.

No, he was not Ivor. He was not Dylan or Ianto or any one of a dozen men to whom she had made love in her life.

But his kisses were the best and she wanted more.

So she impetuously yanked him to her and boldly kissed him again, enjoying his surprise and the passion she knew she roused within him.

She would show Trystan why most men liked her.

He broke away, panting. "You should behave like a decent woman and go home to bed."

She put her hands on his broad chest, feeling the taut muscles and the thudding of his heart through his tunic. "I can do what I wish. I am a grown woman."

She reached for the lacing at the neck of his soft woolen tunic, pulled the knot loose and slipped her hand inside the shirt beneath to stroke his naked flesh.

"I can tell," he replied huskily, his hand boldly caressing her breast through the silk of her garment and her thin shift.

She pulled her hand away, but only to slip it up and under his tunic and shirt. She wanted to feel even more of his body.

His breathing grew raw as he pressed another heated kiss upon her willing lips. She parted them, allowing his tongue to slip inside the waiting warmth.

He moved her back against the wall and then she realized he was undoing the lacing at the back of her gown as he continued to kiss her.

No, he was not like any other man. She had always guessed it would be so.

Why not find out everything?

As she continued to stroke his chest, the lacing of her bodice gave way. With impassioned impatience, he tugged it lower, and eagerly she thrust her breasts toward him. When he took her nipple between his lips, she nearly cried out with delight at the sensations he aroused. Only the vague realization that the guard might hear kept her silent.

Needing more, desperate for more, she ground her hips against him.

Giving him permission. Asking him. Wanting him.

She reached beneath his tunic to find the drawstring of his breeches.

Panting, he positioned her against the wall and shoved her skirt up, then lifted her, his strong hands on her naked buttocks.

"Yes, oh yes," she whispered as she gripped his shoulders and wrapped her legs around his waist.

Then, with frantic, fervent urgency, he took her.

Biting her lip to keep from crying out in ecstasy, she welcomed every powerful thrust. The tension built in delicious anticipation, seeming to stretch like the string of a lute being tuned.

And he was like a master minstrel who knew precisely how to play upon her body as if it were an instrument with which he was intimately familiar, until finally the tension snapped and wave after wave of release swept through her.

His breath hot upon her, he made almost no sound at all, even when he finally stiffened, then slumped against her, spent.

She laid her head against his shoulder, exhausted and complete, too, as her breathing slowly returned to normal.

As everything slowly returned to normal.

She had just made love with Trystan DeLanyea, who didn't even like her.

Sickening remorse took the place where passion had ruled moments ago.

He had never liked her, not since they were children and he would come to her father's brewery with the baron, his father. He would simply stand and look at her with his studious eyes as if there was something terribly wrong with her. In desperation she had teased and jeered at him until she got a response, even if what he said had never been pleasing to hear.

She slipped her legs to the ground and pulled away, her skirt falling back into place, covering her nakedness and the evidence of her hasty act.

At nearly the same time, Trystan turned away and retied his breeches, then smoothed down his tunic.

"I'm sorry," he mumbled. "I didn't want to do that."

"Yes, you did," she retorted, her pride pricked by his shamed attitude as she reached back and briskly tied the lacing of her bodice. "If you didn't, you wouldn't have, so don't try to deny it."

He faced her and when he spoke, his tone was grimly determined. "I regret this, and I would rather we both forgot what just happened."

Although she told herself she should not be surprised, hot tears stung Mair's eyes.

But she would die a thousand deaths before she would show any hurt to him.

"What?" she demanded. "What just happened? Nothing at all!"

"I am glad you agree."

"Oh, I agree, all right. Dylan was something, and *this was not*," she sneered.

Then, before he could wound her more with his words, she marched past him and disappeared down the stairs.

As Trystan remained on the wall walk, he sighed and ran his hand through his disheveled, shoulder-length hair. God's wounds, what had come over him? How could he have been so lustful and so stupid?

And with Mair, of all women!

Mair, who always seemed to be laughing at him, as if everything he did was some kind of jest for her amusement and who apparently slept with any man who asked her.

Who had borne his own cousin a son out of wedlock.

God save him, he needed to marry the sweet, innocent Lady Rosamunde, who would surely react with just horror if she heard of his disgraceful, lustful behavior.

He should have controlled himself better, but what man could have resisted Mair's fiery kiss? What other mortal could have walked away when a voluptuous, passionate woman leaned into him with such unabashed desire?

No man he knew, not even Griffydd.

At least he felt remorse for his lascivious act, unlike Mair. If it had been any other woman, she would have fled the moment she realized her mistake after kissing him.

But Mair had not, and so he had naturally given in to the temptation she offered.

Yes, it was her fault for kissing him again, and for being the sort of woman who would wait for a man in such a place, for such a reason. Therefore, he would not berate himself. It had been all Mair's fault.

Nevertheless, it would still create a difficulty if Lady Rosamunde learned about tonight. He must ensure she did not, even if that meant speaking privately to Mair. Considering Mair's anger, he suspected she might be as anxious as he to keep their assignation a secret.

He would go to Mair tomorrow. He would not rush to her first thing, for if he left the castle too early, it might cause comment, and then he would have to make explanations.

He didn't want to have to lie.

Mair's pace quickened as she crossed the wide courtyard. She wanted nothing more than to get home, away from Trystan and the rest of the DeLanyeas, too.

She must have been deranged to make love to him!

And him—he had some gall, that one, trying to make her feel ashamed for what was only natural. She was proud to be the mother of Dylan's son, and everybody knew how Trystan had mooned about over Dylan's wife, Genevieve.

A sardonic smile lifted the corners of her lips. It seemed Trystan was over that particular infatuation.

"Mair!"

A male shape appeared near the gate moving toward her, armed and wearing chain mail. Thick, dark hair brushed brawny shoulders, and the man stood a whole head taller than she.

Ivor.

"Where were you?" she demanded coolly, regarding his angular face in the moonlight.

"Giving the watch the password for the night, I was," he said apologetically as he reached out to take her hands. "Lovely you look in this dress, Mair."

She moved away. "Did you think I would wait forever?"

"Mair," he wheedled in his deep, velvety voice which was really the most attractive thing about him. "Duty it was, and nothing else. Only that would keep me away from you, that and your women's… It's finished, is it?"

"Yes."

"You're not angry because I am a little late, surely? Other women might be, but not you. You are too good to be upset about such a little thing."

She sighed. She had done what she had done, and she would not blame another. "No, I am not angry with you," she replied.

"Glad I am to hear it," Ivor said, dropping his voice to a whisper as she let him take her hand. He started to lead her toward the storerooms. "My barracks are too crowded with celebrating soldiers tonight."

She tugged her hand from his. "I'm tired, Ivor. I am going to go home to bed."

"I can come with you. My duties are finished for tonight. Your son is with Angharad, isn't he?"

"I said I was tired, Ivor. Good night."

Leaving her eager lover dumbfounded and standing alone in the moonlight, Mair continued on her way.

The next morning, Baron Emryss DeLanyea gave a prodigious sigh as he limped onto the dais in the great hall of Craig Fawr to join his youngest son in breaking their fast. Other trestle tables had been set up for the feeding of the servants and guests, and a bevy of maidservants hastened to put out the first meal of the day.

"God save me!" the baron said with a grunt as he sat heavily. "The wind must be from the east, my leg is aching so!"

He turned toward Trystan and ran a scrutinizing gaze over him. "No sleep last night, is it? Was it too much wine, or a woman?"

"Da!" Trystan chided quietly, glancing around at the guests.

Fortunately, the pious Lady Rosamunde had not returned from the chapel, where Trystan had feasted his eyes on her. She had looked like an angel in her gown of pale blue, her bounteous blonde hair only partly hidden by the thinnest of white silk veils. He would have lingered and waited to escort her back to the hall, yet he dreaded appearing too like an eager puppy. As much as he desired her, he wanted to maintain some dignity.

He also thought he would be better able to converse with her after he had spoken with Mair.

"Very well," Baron DeLanyea replied lightly. "Do not tell me. But I would rather it was a woman than wine. I have no patience for drunkards."

"Aye, I know," his son replied, glancing at his father's grinning face.

Then he noticed the shrewd scrutiny lurking in the baron's eye. Half-blind his father may be, but he always saw everything. And if he happened to miss something, his wife did not.

Between his parents, it was almost impossible to keep a secret, Trystan thought, trying not to scowl.

"A woman, then. Well, and you are a young man, so I suppose it is to be expected. Even Griffydd had his—"

"Lovers," Trystan finished impatiently. "And Dylan, of course, and as long as I treat the women well and as a chivalrous man should, no shame to them or me."

When he saw his father's face, Trystan wished he had kept quiet.

"Aye, that's right. And whatever happens is between you and the woman."

This time, Trystan kept his mouth shut.

"I only hope you are dallying with a Welshwoman and not a Norman one," his father remarked quietly as he leaned forward to rip a piece of warm bread from the loaf in front of him.

Mott, his father's favorite hunting hound, and a huge black beast of a dog, sniffed and lumbered forward, obviously expecting some scraps to fall to him.

"Gwen likes you," the baron continued, nodding at the serving wench who was slightly younger than Trystan.

Gwen was pretty, too, and her plump, rounded curves suited her. She was genial and kind, and a man could do worse. Trystan had, in fact, stolen a kiss or two from Gwen in the kitchen, but that was as far as that had gone. "Isn't she going to marry Ianto?"

"Oh, yes, I forgot."

"I didn't, and I am not dallying with anybody."

"No?" His father almost made that sound a sin.

"No!" Trystan frowned. "What's wrong with Norman women? You married one."

His father's response was a low chuckle. "Your mother is exceptional."

Trystan tried to look as if he had not heard this a thousand times. It was no secret his father loved his exceptional mother exceptionally well.

His father grew serious. "Normans are a stern and ambitious lot, most of them," he said, "and they hold their honor dear. It wouldn't be wise to promise more to a Norman woman than you are willing to give."

Trystan grabbed the loaf and tore off a piece, then proceeded to rip it into little bits that fell on the floor to be gobbled up by Mott. "I have made no promises to any woman."

"A word of warning is all, my son," his father said placatingly. "I would not care to have such trouble as Dylan's wedding caused again."

No longer hungry, Trystan shoved back his chair and stood. "Neither do I. I assure you, Da, I will try to conduct myself with wisdom and honor, in all things.''

The baron looked shocked. ''Of course you will, Trystan. I never thought otherwise.''

Trystan didn't answer as he turned on his heel and strode away.

The baron absently scratched Mott's head. ''Thinking I should have a little chat with his mother, me,'' he muttered.

His opinion did not alter as he watched his son halt near the door and flush with apparent pleasure as Lady Rosamunde D'Heureux and her father arrived to break the fast.

Chapter Two

Trystan knew he was blushing like a guilty little boy as he smiled at the lovely Lady Rosamunde, yet he couldn't help it.

Even though it was impossible, he felt as if he must bear some visible sign of his lewd, lustful behavior that would surely disgust this fine, devout young woman.

"Good morning, Sir Trystan," Lady Rosamunde said softly, demurely lowering her eyes— although not before he caught a hint of a pleased smile.

A smile like that would surely never be given to him again if she learned what he had done.

"Greetings, my lady, my lord," he replied, also addressing Lady Rosamunde's short, stout and unremittingly stern father.

Like most Normans, Sir Edward D'Heureux wore his gray hair cut round his head and curled.

This chilly morning he wore a long, dark robe trimmed with fur, and a very displeased expression.

Trystan recalled the rather shocking amount of ale Sir Edward had consumed last night, as well as wine, and wondered if that perhaps accounted for his unpleasant mood. He hoped it was that, and nothing personal.

He darted a surreptitious glance back at his own father, who had always worn his hair to his shoulders and dressed with simplicity. He was still seated on the dais eating, drinking ale, and watching his son and their guests like a hawk. Mercifully, his father was always gracious and charming to guests, so he need have no fear of embarrassment on that score.

"Please, sit at the high table," Trystan invited, determined to ignore his curious parent and wondering if he should cut his own hair, for like his brother and cousin, he emulated the baron in dress and hairstyle.

Sir Edward nodded and marched toward the dais, but Lady Rosamunde laid her soft, gentle hand on Trystan's arm and regarded him pleadingly. "Must we?" she murmured anxiously in her dulcet voice.

"We can sit over there, my lady," Trystan replied with a smile, nodding at another vacant table, and inwardly vastly pleased that she wanted to be as alone with him as a virtuous lady could.

"Oh, thank you," she said as he led the way.

Lady Rosamunde even sat gracefully, moving her skirts aside with a singularly fluid gesture. Again, she looked at him, her blue eyes filled with concern. "I hope you do not take offense, sir, but I find your father rather…intimidating."

Trystan sat close beside her and inhaled the delicate scent of her perfume.

Mair always smelled of honey and spices, the ingredients of mead and *braggot*, a special Welsh brew that was a combination of ale and mead.

But he wouldn't think of Mair now. "There is no need to apologize, my lady. Many people do, especially his enemies."

"I hope you do not count me among your family's enemies!" Lady Rosamunde cried in distress, her cheeks flushing in a most becoming manner.

"Certainly not," Trystan hastened to assure her.

Lady Rosamunde smiled.

It was a very nice smile, even if there was no…

No! There was nothing lacking in her smile. It was a wonderful smile, and this beautiful woman was smiling at him, and he would be glad, and he would stop thinking of Mair's smile and the freckles scattered across her nose and the way her eyes crinkled with delight.

And how they flashed with anger if she was annoyed. Or the mockery in them when she teased him. If only she had stayed annoyed last night!

"I am very glad to hear that we are your friends," Lady Rosamunde continued as Gwen set down bread and ale before her.

The lady paid no attention at all to Gwen.

"I hope this does not mean you are in any hurry to leave us," Trystan said, nodding his thanks to Gwen, who cast a slightly disgruntled glance at Lady Rosamunde, which she did not see.

"Oh, I am in no hurry at all," Lady Rosamunde said.

Glancing about and seeing that nobody was looking their way, not even his father, Trystan dared to reach beneath the table and take her soft, slender hand in his. "Again, I am glad."

With an expression of dismay and doubt, she looked at his hand holding hers.

He was suddenly confused. If she didn't want him to take her hand, why did she not pull it away? Yet if she welcomed this slight familiarity, why did her hand seem so limp and lifeless, and why did her face bear that expression?

It was as if she were displeased, yet lacking the resolve to do anything about it.

So he pulled it back, to spare her any discomfort.

With a shy, even more dubious glance at him, she blushed again.

He began to think himself a fool. She was a

proper, modest maiden. He should not expect her to react boldly, or decisively.

That was a point in her favor, surely.

"The day looks to be fine. Would you care to ride out with me later?" he asked. "With a guard, too, of course," he hastened to add, lest she think he was making an improper suggestion.

"I would be delighted, Sir Trystan," she replied softly.

His heart filled with a sense of pleasant triumph. This woman was a great prize, the epitome of noble Norman womanhood, and there could be no doubt that she liked him, perhaps enough to accept his proposal of marriage.

Wedding Lady Rosamunde would prove his worth to everybody who measured him against Griffydd and Dylan and his father.

Therefore, he must and would win her, and he would make certain nothing prevented it.

"Something was the matter," Emryss DeLanyea said defensively, regarding his placid wife as she sat in the solar. "Looked like he hadn't slept a wink, our Trystan, and touchy as a bear with a thorn in his paw."

"Perhaps he does not like to be interrogated like an errant child. He is a man now, Emryss, after all," Lady Roanna replied with the small, loving smile she reserved for her husband alone as she continued to work on her tapestry.

"He didn't say that," the baron replied as he started to pace, limping as he always did from the wound he had received years ago. "I am no seer to be reading his mind. If he didn't want me to ask, he should have told me."

"And this from a man who lets nobody know when he's troubled," Lady Roanna noted matter-of-factly.

The baron threw himself into his heavy chair, then grinned. "All right, then. He comes by his reticence honestly—but more from you than me."

"Wherever he gets it, he does keep his feelings to himself and always has. Still, I am troubled that he was so unwilling to say why he was tired if there was nothing wrong."

"I'm sure it's a woman."

Roanna frowned. "Do you suppose he was doing something he should not with Lady Rosamunde? I noticed the way he was attending to her and dancing with her at the feast, and she was certainly enjoying it."

Emryss scratched beneath his eye patch. "I hope not," he muttered.

"Don't you like her?"

He shrugged, looking more like a sulking child than the lord of a castle. "Not particularly."

"She's very beautiful."

"I suppose. I was hoping Trystan would have more sense than to be taken in by a pretty face."

"Not every man can be wise. Indeed, you were much older than Trystan is now when you met me, or you might have been swayed by beauty and married somebody else."

"All these years, my love, and you still cannot believe that you are beautiful."

"Only to you, my darling, and that is more than enough," she replied with another little smile. She grew serious again. "You think he is being taken in by Lady Rosamunde? That she doesn't really care for him?"

Again, her husband shrugged. "I don't know. She's too...too demure. Too delicate. Too perfect. Something has to be wrong."

"Because she seems perfect, or because she has captured Trystan's fancy?"

"I suppose she seems perfect if you want a wife without a hint of life. By the saints, I'm always surprised to realize she's actually breathing. There's no spark, no vital fire in her at all."

"If Trystan was with her last night, maybe she hides her spark save for a handsome young man who has captured her heart."

"You're assuming she has a heart to capture," her husband muttered. "God's wounds, Roanna, I hope to God he wasn't with her. I don't need to have another enraged nobleman complaining that a young man in my charge has deflowered his daughter and demanding that they marry."

"Emryss," Roanna chided softly. "This is not Dylan we're talking about, or Griffydd. This is Trystan. Do you truly believe he would make love with a Norman woman like Lady Rosamunde before marriage?"

"So if he wasn't with her," the baron mused aloud, "maybe he was with somebody else." A twinkle of amusement appeared in his eye. "Maybe Mair."

Roanna's eyebrows rose. "You didn't suggest that to him, I'm sure."

"Of course not. He probably would have hit me." Emryss grinned ruefully. "But there's a woman with a spark!"

"Unfortunately, I don't think he would ever consider marriage to any woman who is not titled," Roanna observed.

"I've been worried about his ambition," Emryss acknowledged. "I know what too much of that can do to a man."

His wife nodded thoughtfully, likewise remembering Dylan's father. "It is also difficult to be the youngest, I think." She sighed softly. "If only Angharad had never said anything. They got along all right until she told them they were going to be married."

"They fought like cats and dogs!" Emryss protested.

"But it was different. Childish spats."

"Maybe I should—"

"Emryss! You cannot say one word!" Roanna warned. "None of our children like to be given advice without asking—and don't tell me they don't get that from you!"

The baron frowned. "You're right. As always. So I will not say anything. Will you?"

"Emryss!"

Her husband slapped his hands on the arms of his chair and rose abruptly. "God's teeth, Roanna! I want to know if he's serious about that Norman creature or not!"

"Creature seems a little harsh."

"Woman. Female. Whatever. I don't trust her. She simpers."

"To be honest, my love, I don't like her much myself. Perhaps this will be merely a passing fancy."

"God's holy heart, I hope so!"

"Whatever is going on, we must try not to interfere. Trystan is a grown man and we shall have to trust him to do the right and honorable thing, with any woman."

Emryss went to his wife and pulled her into his arms. "I only want him to be happy, Roanna, as happy as we have been."

Roanna's smile touched his heart, as it always did. "I know, my love, I know," she murmured as she reached up to kiss him.

If any of their children had happened to walk into the solar at that particular moment, they would have discovered that passion need never die, even after thirty years of marriage.

"Arthur, don't play with your food. Eat it, or I'll give it to the pig," Mair chided as she added some more wood to the fire in the hearth of the small house where they lived within the encircling walls of the brewery bequeathed to her by her father.

Other buildings thus enclosed included the malt house, the brewery proper, the storehouse and the stable where she kept her horse and wagon. Her business was a prosperous one, because she was very good at her work. And because it was so prosperous, Mair was beholden to no one, and dependent on no man, and she liked it that way.

Her gray eyed boy frowned as he lifted his spoon and let it drop into the sodden mass of cooked oats.

It was no secret to anybody that while her drink was superb, her food was something else.

Mair sniffed at the pot holding the remains of the porridge. For herself, she preferred fruit first thing in the morning. A growing boy, she was sure, needed something that would stick to his ribs.

"I didn't burn it, did I?" she asked warily. It didn't smell burned, but then, she wasn't trying to eat it.

"No, it's fine," Arthur muttered.

"You don't have to finish the rest of it," Mair said. "If you like, you can have an apple from the bowl, but only one, mind. I'll need the rest for a treat I'm making for supper—or that I'll try to," she finished with a self-deprecating smile.

"Oh. Is that Ivor coming for dinner again?"

"Perhaps *that Ivor* is," she replied, "and if he does, don't you be rude to him."

She felt a twinge of guilt, for she had been far more than rude to Ivor last night. The least she could do after her terrible mistake, she had decided, would be to offer him a meal, as well as welcome him to her bed. They had not been together for days.

Maybe that was why she had found it so difficult to control her desire with Trystan.

If she were an animal, perhaps, she reminded herself. Some priests tried to preach that women were the embodiment of sinful temptation from Eve onward, but she would not use that excuse, either. She had wanted Trystan DeLanyea last night, and she had had him.

Now she had to live with that decision, hasty

and stupid though it was. At least she and Ivor were not pledged to each other in any way, and for that she was very thankful.

Really very thankful, she suddenly realized.

"I won't be rude," Arthur mumbled. He started to tap his spoon against his bowl.

Mair left the hearth and gave him a studious look. He was upset about something, or he would not be lingering here.

"Did you have a good time with Trefor and Angharad?" she asked.

Bang went Arthur's spoon. "I *hate* Trefor!"

Condemning herself for letting her own concerns blind her to her son's distress, Mair wiped her hands on her skirt and sat opposite Arthur. "What happened? What did Trefor do?"

"He said that I had better be nice to him, or he would tell our father not to make me a knight when I am grown."

Mair sighed. "He's said things like that before, and didn't your da tell you Trefor was wrong? Hasn't he *promised* that you will be a knight, if you do all that you should?"

Arthur gripped the spoon so tightly his knuckles went white. "Yes."

"Then you mustn't let Trefor upset you. He does it to annoy you and make you angry. That makes him feel powerful. If you want him to stop, just laugh when he makes these foolish threats."

"I try, but he's so…so…"

"So Trefor?" Mair suggested with a sympathetic smile. "I know, my son. There are some people who can anger us without even trying."

Like Trystan.

"I don't like Ivor, either."

"Why not? Isn't he nice to you?"

Arthur shrugged, his action so like that of all the DeLanyea men that she would have smiled, if not for what had happened last night. "I don't think you like him much, either," her son observed.

"Of course I do!"

"Does he want to marry you?" Arthur demanded.

Mair rose and went to stir the porridge again. Unfortunately, it was now of the consistency of hardened mud. "I don't know."

"You can't."

Suspecting Trefor hadn't been the only one saying things last night, she cast a wary glance at Arthur over her shoulder as she lifted the porridge pot from the hook.

Angharad really had to keep her mouth shut about her stupid prophecy that she would marry Trystan. "Why not? If I love him, why shouldn't I?"

"Because I don't like him."

"Arthur, I don't want to marry anybody," she said truthfully. "I enjoy Ivor's company, that's all, and he enjoys mine. There's nothing wrong with that.''

"Am I going back to Angharad's tonight?''

"Not if you don't want to.''

"I don't want to.''

"Then you don't have to.'' She went to her son and ruffled his dark hair that was so like his father's. "Arthur, you're my darling, precious son, and nothing will ever change that. I promise.''

Arthur blushed as he always did when she said such things and regarded her with a slightly condemning look that he sometimes made when he thought she was embarrassing him—and that was suddenly very familiar.

Anwyl, how could she never have seen his resemblance to Trystan DeLanyea before?

Hadn't Trystan looked at her with that expression a hundred times, and as recently as last night?

"Arthur,'' she said, glad her voice didn't betray her sudden surprise, "why don't you go to the smithy and watch Ianto work awhile? Or would you rather help me in the brewery?''

"Oh, the smithy, Mam!'' Arthur cried as his face lit up with a grin—his father's grin, which had none of Trystan's dour reticence about it. "Ianto's doing swords today!''

Her son jumped up from the table and ran to the door.

"Come back when the sun sets!'' she called out

after him, hoping that he heard and would not be late.

She would prefer to have some company when Ivor came, until she was more herself.

She bent down to pick up the pot to take the rest of the hardening porridge out to the pig before she got to her work.

When she straightened, she saw Ivor standing on the threshold, a smile on his face. "Ivor! I didn't expect to see you this morning."

"I came to apologize again for being late last night."

"I'm sorry I was so abrupt with you."

"Ah." He went to her and wrapped his brawny arms around her waist, then kissed her neck.

"Ivor! I am trying to work!"

"And I am telling you how much I've missed you."

"Well, you missed me in your bed."

"Mair!"

"I'm sorry, Ivor. Just tired I am."

"I thought perhaps you missed me, too."

She wouldn't lie, so she merely shrugged and kept her gaze focused on the chain mail covering his broad chest. "Shouldn't you be leading a patrol of the wood or the road?"

"I am to escort Trystan and Lady Rosamunde riding in a bit, when the lady's ready. I thought there would be enough time for a little visit with you.''

''How much time?''

He chuckled softly. ''Not enough for that, I'm sorry to say.''

Mair tried to look disappointed and hoped she succeeded. Ivor was a good man and had done nothing to merit her relief that he couldn't stay. ''He likes the lady, does he?''

''Can't take his eyes from her, him. Like a love-sick lad.'' Ivor's voice lowered to a whisper as he caressed her breast. ''Or like me when I'm near you.''

She gently removed his hand. ''Should you not go back?''

Ivor chuckled softly. ''A man in love himself will understand if I dally.''

''You had best be dutiful.'' She put a smile on her face. ''Can you sup with Arthur and me tonight?''

''Nothing would make me happier.'' He grinned, reminding her why she had taken him to her bed in the first place. ''Well, one or two other things.'' He let go of her and went toward the door with obvious reluctance. ''And I promise I won't be late.''

''Don't be,'' she replied with more genuine good humor.

She watched him leave. Yes, he was a good man, but she didn't love him. She never would.

Sighing, she glanced down at the pot of porridge. As she regarded the awful-looking mess, she made a rueful grin. Why was it she could make the best ale and mead in Wales, and yet failed with something as apparently simple as porridge?

"One of the mysteries of life, I suppose," she muttered as she bent to pick up the pot again.

She heard a sound at the door and glanced up, wondering if Arthur had returned, or Ivor.

Instead, a grave and grim Trystan stood in her doorway.

Chapter Three

The morning breeze had ruffled Trystan's shoulder-length hair, and he was dressed in a fine, dark wool tunic belted about the waist which emphasized his muscular shoulders and chest. Silhouetted as he was in the sunlight, she couldn't help noticing he had the best legs of all the DeLanyea men, including Dylan.

Immediately she remembered the strength of him as the memory of his powerful, passionate embrace flashed into her mind.

Nevertheless, her first instinct was to tell him to go away. She didn't want to talk to him, any more than she wanted to recall what had happened between them last night.

Lifting her chin defiantly, Mair tilted her head to regard Trystan coldly.

"What do you want?" she demanded, pleased that she could sound so calm when her heart was beating like a minstrel's tabor during a fast-paced dance.

"May I come in?" Trystan asked, not moving from the threshold.

"I hear you are taking Lady Rosamunde out riding this morning, whenever she can get herself ready. Surprised, me, she's willing to leave the castle, or has the strength to stay on a horse. Looks like she needs a few good meals, her. All skin and bones and too pale by far."

"I did not come here to discuss Lady Rosamunde. May I come inside?" Trystan repeated with grave courtesy.

"You came in right well last night, so I could hardly deny you entry to my house today, could I?"

"Of course you could refuse," he said with a scowl, "and as an honorable knight, I would respect your wishes."

"Come in, Sir Trystan, and welcome," she replied sarcastically.

As he sauntered into her house like a conquering warrior, she told herself to pay no heed to his reactions. He had always been a cold, prudish fellow, and that was not her fault. To be sure, they had made a mistake last night, but it was not the end of the world.

He circled her table, then stopped, apparently fascinated by the ruined porridge.

"I must say you surprise me," she remarked, trying to draw his attention from her failure and commanding herself not to blush. Everybody knew she was no cook, so let him stare as if he had never seen ruined porridge before.

He raised his serious eyes to regard her steadily.

"I am surprised you would deign to come to my house." She didn't move away as he silently came closer. "Well, Sir Trystan, what do you want?"

"I came to ask you..." He hesitated a moment, and she felt a moment's pleasure at his discomfort. It served him right for his arrogant mien. "Have you told anyone about...?"

"About last night?" she supplied when he fell awkwardly silent. "What do you think I would say?"

He gave her an angry, frustrated look as if what they had done was all her fault. "Knowing you, it could be almost anything."

"Oh, so you think you know me?"

"Of course."

Smiling, she leaned closer and said, "Maybe I told everybody I met that I had just made love with Trystan DeLanyea on the wall walk."

He crimsoned as he crossed his arms over his chest and glared at her. "You didn't."

"How do you know? That would be the truth, wouldn't it?" she noted as she strolled around the table, so that it stood between them.

"Have you no shame?" he demanded. "Doesn't what we did last night trouble you?"

"Nothing much about me seemed to trouble you last night—at least not when we were in each other's arms."

"As I said last night, it was a mistake."

"And I agreed. So why are you here now?"

Trystan cleared his throat. "I have plans, Mair," he said, looking at her with his stern, determined gray eyes. "Plans that do not include you."

A pain unlike anything Mair had ever felt before—a pain that was not physical, but seemingly pure feeling—welled up inside her. She beat it back, willed it away, told herself she had known this all along.

"I am going to marry Lady Rosamunde D'Heureux, if she will do me the honor of accepting my hand."

"My plans do not include you, either," Mair replied, telling herself she didn't care about his plans, certainly not if he truly wanted to wed that Norman statue of a woman who looked about as pleasant to bed as a piece of marble. "That is why I have said nothing. To anybody."

Trystan sighed as if a great weight had been taken from his shoulders. "Mair," he said in a softer voice as he approached her, "I'm sorry for what happened. I truly don't know what came over me."

Mair didn't move away from him. She couldn't. All her energy was needed to keep her voice level and her hands from trembling.

"I acted like a lustful, loathsome beast," he continued sadly.

"You acted like a man who was with a willing woman, that's all. I...I'm sorry I compared you to Dylan."

His expression compelled her to go on in a breathless rush. "I am not ashamed of being his lover, and he was marvelous, but..."

Trystan's eyes suddenly seemed to lighten, as if from within. "But?"

She couldn't meet his gaze.

He moved still closer, so that she could feel his breath hot on her cheek. "Have a care, Mair, or I will be getting conceited."

"I think you have plenty enough to be modest about," she replied, trying to sound defiant or flippant, or anything but anxious for his kiss.

"I know that there are those who compare me unfavorably to my brother and cousin and father."

As she stared into his familiar eyes, she suddenly saw a vulnerability there she had never suspected existed.

How would it feel to have such older relations to be compared with? A father as famous as Emryss DeLanyea, who had lost an eye but survived the Crusade and all that came after? Or grim

Griffydd, who all respected and trusted? Or even Dylan, who was the envy of men everywhere for his charm and looks?

Was it any wonder Trystan wanted a wife like Lady Rosamunde, the very personification of Norman womanhood, the beauty of a powerful family?

"You have much to be proud of, too," she finally said.

His mouth curved up in a slow, incredibly attractive smile. "I do?"

"You know you do," she snapped, moving so that the table was between them again. She needed a barrier if he was going to look at her like that.

"Like what? I have a fine father and brother and cousin."

"You surely know your own merits without me having to tell you." She swallowed hard as he started to come round the table. She was tempted to flee her own house, but he was between her and the door. "You have plans, Trystan, and I am not in them."

At last he came to a halt only a step from her.

But he didn't leave. Instead, he looked at her as if he had never really seen her before. "What about you, Mair? What plans do you have?"

No one had ever asked her that in her life, and indeed, she hadn't thought about such a question herself. "I...um...why, to see Arthur grow to be a fine young knight, and to make the best ale I can," she stammered.

Very gently he reached out and took her shoulders in his strong hands. "Is that all?" he asked softly as he pulled her into his arms, another emotion smoldering in his gray eyes. His breathing quickened, matching the rapid rhythm of her own.

"Take your hands off me, Trystan," she whispered.

In a way, he did, for his hold loosened.

Then he slowly moved his hands down her arms in a gesture that was more like a caress than anything else. "Order me to go, Mair, and I will."

As his fingers began another slow, tantalizing journey, Mair couldn't ask him to leave.

How could she, when she desperately wanted him to stay and make love with her again? How often had she dreamed of being in his embrace, just like this? How many nights had she drifted off to sleep wondering what it would be like to have Trystan beside her?

What would she not have given to have had him for her first lover?

Everything but her pride, her pride that made her keep her desire for him a secret for so long.

And now…now she was where she had so often longed to be.

And she did not want him to go.

Instead, she accepted her desire and eagerly gave in to the yearning within her.

His long hair brushed against her bare arms as she wound them about his neck. His chest pressed against her breasts, the sensation incredibly exciting.

Then his mouth was upon hers in a savage, wildly arousing kiss.

It was even better than before. Last night, he had been all primitive passion and fiery lust. Today, there was that—and more besides.

Today, he seemed to be holding back, more tentative, more aware of her and what she might want.

What she wanted was him inside her, loving her. Completing her. Making her feel as if he needed her as she needed him.

She had no time for hesitant tenderness, no need for softly spoken words of encouragement, no patience for gentle caresses.

She thrust her tongue between his lips and into his warm mouth as her hands sought his arousal. She stroked him boldly, at the same time twisting and turning as he ran his hands over her willing body.

With increasing need, she ground her hips against him and gloried in the low, rolling growl that burst from his throat.

She pulled him down to the packed earth floor.

Kneeling between her legs, he kissed her and fondled her breasts as she herself tugged up her skirt.

He took an instant to untie his breeches—and then he was inside her, filling her, giving her almost unbearable pleasure. She held to him tightly as she arched to meet him, need answering need.

Never had she felt more attuned to a lover, as if their union had been preordained and so must be perfect. How else could he know that licking the hollow of her throat thrilled her so, or that softly brushing the underside of her breast with his fingertips made her nearly faint with pleasure?

Clutching his shoulders, she raised herself to suck the tender lobe of his ear into her mouth. His breath caught as she took it gently between her teeth.

In another heartbeat she had to let it go, for she was fast approaching the peak.

All too soon, it was as if she had leapt from a high place onto clouds of unbelievable pleasure. So immersed was she in her own enjoyment, it took her a moment to realize he had reached that after-place, too.

Panting, he lay his head on her breasts while she stroked his curling dark hair. She ignored the hardness of the floor, which she had not noticed before.

"God's wounds, Mair, why do you make me do this?" he murmured.

She stiffened slightly. "I don't *make* you do anything."

"You make me give in to the basest elements of my nature," he said with what sounded like genuine regret as he rose and began to fix his unkempt clothing.

When she scrambled to her feet he regarded her as if she were some kind of siren, luring him to his doom. "I am only a man, after all, and a man has needs—"

Mair's expression hardened. She had not enticed him here; he had come of his own free will. She had not touched him first. She had not drugged him, or gotten him drunk.

She had done nothing wrong—nothing except give in to her desire and believe he cared for her. "Your needs, is it? Let me guess. That Norman you're sniffing round will not let you touch her, so you come to me. I will not be a substitute for any woman, Trystan DeLanyea!"

"Mair, I did not come for such a disgusting purpose," he growled as he, too, got to his feet and fixed his clothing. He gave her a sharp, condemning look. "If you think me capable of such a motive, I am surprised you let me touch you."

With swift, aggressive motions, she adjusted her disheveled bodice. "No more surprised than I. Now get out!"

"Not until I have your word that you will keep

what has happened between us a secret." He flushed. "Both times."

She looked at him as she might a mouse who had gotten into her stores. "You are wise to be worried about what I'll tell Ivor tonight—when we're in bed!"

Trystan's hands balled into fists. "I knew you gave your favors freely, Mair, but I never knew just how freely."

She lifted her chin, her fierce eyes flashing. "Go ahead, insult me!" she declared scornfully, full of anger at him, and at herself for being weak and giving in to her desire. "Why not? You hate me, and I hate you. I probably shouldn't tell Ivor anything! That would be admitting that I am mad. I must be, to make love with you. And doubly mad to do it twice. But at least I will not accuse you of making me do something against my will. I chose to do it, I am sorry and it won't happen again— because *I* will not let it!" She put her hands on her hips. "Now leave me, sir, and never come here again. You remind me of my shame."

He made a skeptical face. "I did not think you had it in you to be ashamed of immorality."

Her face flushed. "I am not ashamed of making love, man!" she snarled. "I am ashamed of making love with *you!* Now get out of my house and never speak to me again!"

Trystan's face was nearly as red as he bowed stiffly and marched to the door.

Mair picked up the porridge pot and threw it after him. It hit the doorframe with a heavy thud, making a large dent, before it rolled on the ground.

She stared at it a moment before she realized the porridge didn't spill because it was too hard. With trembling hands, she picked it up, then forced herself to survey the dent.

If that pot had struck Trystan, she could have killed him.

She almost wished she had. Almost.

Nevertheless, she silently vowed, she would never go near him again, that Trystan with his fine, muscular body and handsome face and eyes that seemed to say...

No, she would have nothing more to do with him, even if he looked at her that way, and even though his hands seemed able to touch and arouse her as no other man, and despite his kisses that filled her such incredible desire...

"Fool," she whispered as she headed for the pigsty. "Stupid, stupid fool!"

She was not referring to Trystan.

From her luxuriously appointed bedchamber in the west tower of Craig Fawr, Lady Rosamunde looked down into the bustling courtyard below. Her idle gaze fell on the tall, brawny captain of the guard as he spoke to his men in that preposterous Welsh. He was not an unattractive fellow, in a rough-hewn, barbaric way. He probably loved his women roughly, too, she thought, the idea warming her.

Nevertheless, he was a barbarian, when all was said and done, and she would not waste her time in useless contemplation of him. Instead, she turned her thoughts to Trystan DeLanyea, who she was keeping waiting for a little while before they went out riding.

A wise woman let a man wait, to increase his anticipation.

She looked out over the wall to the land beyond the comfortable fortress which, surprisingly, would have done any Norman proud. Then she surveyed her bedchamber.

The comfortable bed had soft, silken coverings, and fine wax candles provided illumination at night. There was a brazier for warmth, and a lovely ewer and basin on the table nearby. There was even a carpet on the floor, a thing only the wealthiest of nobles possessed.

Still, how could any intelligent, sophisticated person want to live so far from London and the court, or anything remotely civilized? As for the local peasants, they were like savages, with their odd language and strange customs, and their disgusting familiarity with their overlord.

Why, she had even heard that that woman in the lovely red gown at the feast was no more than an alewife—and yet she had danced as if she were…as if she were somebody.

Well, Rosamunde thought contentedly as she turned back to look into the courtyard again, surely it would be easy for a woman as beautiful and graceful as she to convince a loving young husband that any man with any ambition at all should spend most of the year in London, near the court.

And she had come to the conclusion that her loving young husband should be handsome Trystan DeLanyea.

Trystan DeLanyea's personal attributes were, of course, but a pleasant bonus to the real issues that did, and should, concern a woman of her rank. The most important thing was wealth and the power that went with it. Without that, a handsome face was nothing, and a comely man's love even less important. Fortunately, everything around her and everything she had seen at Craig Fawr attested to the DeLanyeas' wealth.

To be sure, there was the problem of Trystan DeLanyea's Welsh blood. Fortunately, he was but one quarter Welsh and the rest Norman. Besides— and as her father was sure to realize eventually, as she had immediately—Trystan's father's ancestry had apparently proved no impediment to the baron's success in an England ruled by Normans.

In fact, given all that she had seen here of the baron's wealth and influence, she was quite certain Sir Trystan DeLanyea was worth marrying. It was regrettable he was not the eldest son, yet she was sure that any son of Baron DeLanyea would be granted a fine and prosperous estate.

Another important factor in her decision was her conviction that Trystan DeLanyea already loved her. She knew men well enough to recognize the signs of infatuation, and it had taken so little effort, she was certain she could ensure that his infatuation lasted longer than most bridegroom's.

Pleased with her rational and wise decision, Rosamunde smiled with the satisfaction often seen on a feline face. Then, thinking she had kept her future husband waiting long enough, she pulled her light cloak about her shoulders and swept from the bedchamber.

Unaware that his fate was apparently decided in a way quite different from Angharad's method, Trystan mentally berated himself for a fool as he marched toward the stables.

How could he have done that—again? How could he have been so weak and filled with lust?

It had to be Mair's fault. No other woman had that effect on him, not even Lady Rosamunde. Why, one look from Mair, one touch of her hands, and he was suddenly powerless to overrule his lust.

Even now, simply thinking about her, and despite what they had just done, he was filled with desire to be with her again.

He rammed his fist into his palm. He wasn't a fool, and he wasn't a love-struck youth, and he could be strong. He must be strong if he was to win Lady Rosamunde.

All he had to do was stay away from Mair. He wouldn't get within twenty yards of her if he could help it, he silently vowed.

He sighed raggedly and ran his hand through his hair. God's wounds, what was wrong with him that he felt this undeniable doubt that he would be able to do even that much?

Maybe nothing, his mind replied. As Mair had so angrily suggested, maybe he was merely a vital young man needing an outlet for his natural urges. He hadn't been to a brothel in weeks and had never particularly enjoyed visiting such places, with their earthy women and filthy sheets.

"Lady Rosamunde!" he cried as he nearly collided with her.

She moved back, smiling shyly. "I didn't mean to startle you, sir."

How lovely she was, with her light blue silken cloak and gossamer white scarf that brushed her cheek.

She wasn't too pale today, for the cool air and

her shy surprise had brought a most becoming pink flush to her face.

"Forgive me for being lost in my thoughts," he said.

"I hope they were not troubling ones."

He smiled and decided this was as good a time as any to make his wishes known. "Not troubling, but important," he replied, "and you were in them."

"I?" she said with modest surprise and a pleasure he was happy to see.

"Yes." He glanced around the busy courtyard where servants and tenants came and went. "Would you come with me to my mother's garden? There is something I would ask you."

She looked around worriedly. "With you? Alone? I thought we were going riding."

"We can do that afterward, my lady. Please come with me to the garden. I assure you, I will not do anything improper."

"Oh, I know you will not, but others might not believe that if we are seen."

"They will if I say so."

Her eyes widened a little, and he regretted sounding so forceful. "If you would rather not, or if you would care to fetch your maid...?" he offered, albeit reluctantly.

The lady smiled and shook her head. "There is no need for that. I trust you, sir."

Her words should have made him proud and happy, and he told himself they would have, if they had not also filled him with even more remorse for being with Mair again.

He held out his arm and after Lady Rosamunde placed her delicate hand upon it, he led her to a bench in his mother's rose garden, now prepared for the coming winter. She sat on the wooden bench he brought her to, in one of the more secluded areas of the garden. He didn't want any servants to hear him propose marriage. Out of respect for her concern about propriety, however, he left the gate open.

"This garden must be very lovely in the summer," Lady Rosamunde noted with a smile. "An oasis in the wilderness."

"It is. But Wales is not so much of a wilderness."

"It is far from London," Lady Rosamunde replied. "For a man of your talents, it must be frustrating to be so far from court."

He smiled. "My talents?"

She flushed prettily. "We have heard of your prowess in tournaments, Sir Trystan. Indeed, you are quite famous, I think."

A rush of pride filled him at her sincere compliment. He had dared to dream that some of the

Norman nobility had heard of his victories, and now it appeared that dream had not been a vain one.

She continued to regard him with wide-eyed wonder. "I am sure any one of my father's friends at court would be delighted to have you as his liege man."

"I wish I could be as certain of that, my lady, as you seem to be," he replied softly as he sat beside her.

"I grant you, having Welsh blood is something of a drawback, but I am sure they would be willing to overlook that."

Trystan's pleasure decreased, for she spoke as if he was seriously tainted, despite his prowess in tournaments and his own family's title. "It is true that I am one-quarter Welsh."

"It is also true your father is well-respected." She gave him a shy, sidelong glance. "I am sure *many* people do not care about your heritage at all."

He told himself she did not mean any insult as he took her thin, cool hand in his. "Do you care about it?"

"No."

Now was the time to ask for her hand, his mind commanded. Now he must speak. Now he should ask her to be his wife.

The words stuck in his throat as she looked at him expectantly.

Again his mind ordered him to ask her to make him the happiest man in Britain by consenting to be his wife.

Instead, he put his arm around her and drew her close for a gentle kiss.

Her lips were as cool as her hands. It was like kissing a rock.

"Forgive me, my lady. Your beauty..." he stammered as he moved away.

He couldn't even finish the excuse.

To his immediate relief, she smiled and did not look overly dismayed. "I am not angry, sir. Indeed, I am flattered, although your action was rather improper."

Despite the coolness of her kiss, he should marry Lady Rosamunde. He should have a place at court, or at least in the entourage of a powerful lord. Marrying into her family would make that possible.

Besides, she was the most beautiful woman who had ever come to Craig Fawr, as well as the most demure, virtuous and graceful. By wedding her, he would have bested Griffydd and Dylan and all the unmarried Norman noblemen in Britain for all the world to see.

And still the words would not come.

"What did you want to ask me, sir?" Lady

Rosamunde said as she delicately adjusted the hood of her cloak.

"How long will you and your father stay at Craig Fawr?"

If the lady was disappointed, her face did not betray her. "At least another fortnight. My father wishes to learn more of your father's silver mining, and his agreement with the Gall-Gaidheal to the north. My father wants to widen the market for our wool and is curious about the bargain the baron struck with Diarmad MacMurdoch." She gave him a coy, sidelong glance. "I hope your father doesn't plan to marry another one of his sons to a Gall-Gaidheal woman."

"No, he does not."

"I am glad to hear it."

"Are you?"

"Very."

Once more he put his arm around her shoulder. "Lady Rosamunde, has any man spoken to you of marriage?" he asked, gently pulling her closer.

"One or two," she admitted.

"Yet you are not married or betrothed?"

"No."

So she did not kiss with fierce and hungry passion like Mair, he thought as he leaned down to kiss Lady Rosamunde. So what if Lady Rosamunde kept her lips as firmly closed as a locked chastity belt.

Lady Rosamunde kissed like a lady, not like a…a woman.

Turning her head away, she broke the kiss. "Sir Trystan, you quite take my breath away," she murmured, her beautiful breasts rising and falling rapidly as if she were indeed breathless.

"Perhaps we should go riding now," Trystan said, standing and holding out his hand, "before I am tempted to act in an impetuous, ungentlemanly manner."

In truth, he had never felt less like acting in an impetuous, ungentlemanly manner.

That was surely all Mair's fault, too. If he had not been with Mair today, he could ask beautiful Lady Rosamunde to be his wife.

But before he did that, for her sake and his, he would find a way to purge his mind and his body of his unholy, distracting lust for Mair.

Chapter Four

"Well, what did he say?" Sir Edward D'Heureux demanded as he watched his daughter brush her long, golden hair later that day. "Did he propose marriage?"

"Not yet," she replied calmly. "But he will."

"How can you be so sure?" her frustrated parent asked as he started to pace.

"I let him kiss me."

Her father came to an abrupt halt. "You what?"

Rosamunde made a smug and satisfied smile as she glanced at him in her mirror. "No need to stare so, Father. I let him kiss me. A very chaste kiss it was, too, but enough to render him speechless. So you need have no fear. Sir Trystan DeLanyea will ask for my hand before we have to leave this godforsaken wasteland."

"God's wounds, I wish I could be so sure!"

Her expression hardened. "I see no need for

haste in this matter. It costs us nothing to enjoy the baron's hospitality, just as we have been living off the hospitality of others since you gambled away the last of my mother's money.''

She smiled sweetly as she went back to brushing her hair with brisk, aggressive strokes. ''And you should bless your luck, such as it is, that I learned about this Welsh custom of paying a bride-price, or *amober,* or however you pronounce it in their ludicrous tongue. I am surely worth a great sum.

''So rest assured, Father, Trystan DeLanyea will marry me and pay well for the privilege. For my dowry, all you need do is give up a few acres of land near London that you never visit anyway. That, and sell your only daughter.''

''Rosamunde, I—''

''I do not need to hear your expressions of remorse and regret yet again, Father.'' She twisted on her stool to regard him steadily. ''I understand my duty, and I shall do it. What do his parents think of the match?''

''I...I don't know,'' her father mumbled, his head bowed.

Her full and rosy lips twisted with disdain. ''In all my life, I ask you to do one simple thing for me—to discover if the DeLanyeas look on my marriage to their son with favor—and you cannot even manage that.''

''It's not my fault,'' Sir Edward whined. ''His

father smiles and talks and never really says anything, no matter how I hint. And that wife of his! She's a veritable clam!''

His manner changed to one of eager hopefulness. ''They have not spoken against it, or made mention of any other prospects. What could they possibly find objectionable about you, my sweet daughter? And Trystan seems to be a good man, Rosamunde. I am sure he will make you happy.''

Rosamunde ignored her father's empty compliment. ''He will worship the ground I tread, and so he will do whatever I ask of him. That is the important thing,'' she muttered as she turned away from her father, who would have sold her one way or another, whether he was rich or poor.

He was a greedy glutton who had pursued his own pleasures all his life, without one thought to his wife or his daughter until the day he ran out of money and realized the most valuable thing he possessed was the flesh of his flesh.

But Rosamunde was no fool. Her beautiful mother had been, praying and hoping for her husband's return whenever he was off gambling and sporting with his worthless cronies and selfish whores. Her mother had been too stupid and blind to see that love was a self-inflicted, weakening folly, a romantic notion dreamed up by troubadors as a means to make their living.

She would not fall into that trap. She would

marry the man her mind told her would be the least likely to gamble, or to sport with other women, or to ignore his wife, even if that meant marrying a man she did not love, who did not stir her in any way except as a means to an end.

Nevertheless, she would bear him children, sons to protect her in her old age, and daughters to marry to other powerful men. She would create a dynasty.

She would never again feel helpless and at the mercy of a man's selfish desires.

As for her desires... The memory of the captain of the guard invaded her thoughts momentarily.

Just as quickly she banished him. She was surely stronger than any physical craving.

She must be.

"Are you sure about this?" her father asked softly. "He is part Welsh, after all—"

Rosamunde jumped to her feet and glared at him. "How dare you question my choice?" she demanded angrily.

"But Lord Kirkheathe is a pure Norman—"

Her expression grew so fierce, it is doubtful many people would have recognized her at that moment.

"Didn't you understand me? The Welsh pay for their brides, and if you want a penny of my marriage portion, you will keep that stupid mouth of yours shut except to eat and drink and do what I say!''

"Forgive me, Rosamunde," he whispered.

"Late for that now, isn't it, Father?" she said scornfully as she regarded him as she might a bug she was about to squash. "You never asked my mother's pardon. Indeed, you never even thought of her before she died."

"I—"

"Leave me, Father. I have to make myself look my best for Trystan DeLanyea, for I must and shall make him marry me."

"Good night, Arthur," Ivor said as the boy headed toward the ladder leading to the loft where he slept.

Her back to them both as she put away the last of the stew, Mair listened to her son's mumbled response and subdued a weary sigh.

It had been all too obvious during the meal that Arthur did not like or approve of Ivor, who was doing his boisterous best to be genial and entertaining.

"I enjoyed that stew, Mair," Ivor observed. "And naturally your ale is always the best. They're going to be needing more up at the castle soon, I should think. After all the feasting, surely they've used just about all you sent before. You'll be a rich woman one day, Mair, especially if they have more guests like Edward D'Heureux. For a Norman, he's got quite a taste for ale.''

"Edward D'Heureux. That would be the beautiful Lady Rosamunde's father?''

"Aye, and a Norman to the bone, save his taste for ale. I think if he ever smiled, his face would break.''

Mair grinned at the captain, who sat at the table as if he belonged there, while she gathered up the dirty spoons. In the soft glow of the lamp, he was nearly as handsome as Trystan. He was certainly well-muscled, and didn't lack for passion.

But did he belong at the head of her table? Did any man? Or was she better off as she had always been, alone and independent?

"Lady Rosamunde smiles, I suppose,'' she remarked.

"Oh, indeed, at Trystan especially, and he smiles back like a besotted ninny. I'm surprised they haven't announced a betrothal yet, although I could see that Sir Edward might not favor anybody with Welsh blood.''

Mair plunged the spoons in a bucket of water and swiftly rinsed them off.

"We've had our laughs at Sir Edward's expense, though, the lads and I. Dafydd came up with some right choice names for him and said them in his hearing.''

"In Welsh, of course,'' Mair noted, glad the

subject was no longer Trystan and Lady Rosamunde as she put the spoons away.

"He must be some angry having to go to Griffydd with that wool."

"Who?"

"Trystan. Leaving in the morning, he is, with ten men of the guard." Ivor's voice lowered and she heard him stand. "Not me, though."

"I wonder why he's going. He doesn't usually—"

She jumped as Ivor put his arms around her waist. "*Anwyl*, Mair, you started like a deer hearing beaters in the bush. What's got into you?" Ivor murmured as he nuzzled the nape of her neck.

She knew he didn't mean anything specific, yet she blushed nonetheless. "You startled me, that's all."

"I've waited all night to be able to hold you."

"Let me finish tidying up," she muttered, gently pushing aside his hands.

Ivor chuckled softly as he moved away. "Never seen you so anxious to clean, me."

"Yes, well, there's no need for hurrying for anything else, is there? Or do you have to be back early tonight?" she asked, busying herself with banking the hearth fire for the night.

"I don't have to be back to the barracks till dawn."

Mair gulped. Maybe she should tell him about
Trystan.

What about Trystan? That they had coupled like
a pair of wild animals, twice?

Why make trouble? She wasn't going to go near
Trystan again, unless she couldn't help it.

No, no, she could help it. She would help it. She
must help it, because he had his ambitious plans
that did not include her.

So what was it about Trystan DeLanyea that still
made his approval seem like the Holy Grail to her?

"I think the baron's sent him away to cool his
head a bit," Ivor remarked behind her. "He hides
it well, but I'm thinking he has no great affection
for Sir Edward, or his daughter."

Mair fought to subdue any pleasure that thought
brought her. "And Lady Roanna? What does she
think?"

"Who can say about that?"

"Aye. Do you think Trystan's ardor for Lady
Rosamunde will cool in a few days?"

"I don't care about his ardor, Mair. It's yours
I'm thinking about. Come to bed."

Smiling, she glanced back over her shoulder—
and then nearly set herself alight when she realized
Ivor was in her bed under her coverings and naked,
to judge by the pile of discarded clothing on the
floor beside it.

He smiled seductively. "Enough of that, Mair,"

he said. "It's been too long. Blow out the lamp and come to bed."

As she slowly approached the bed, her hands balled into fists. "Is that an order, captain of the guard?"

"If you would like it to be."

"I do not take orders in my own house, or anywhere."

He looked startled. "I'm sorry, Mair. I'm anxious, is all, and I meant—"

"Yes, you and your desires. I understand. What I need or what I want is of no consequence, is it?"

He sat up, his brow furrowing. "Mair, I want to be with you. Why are you so angry?"

"Do you want to marry me?"

He looked as if she had just threatened to cut off his manhood.

"Marry?" he finally managed to say. "I have never promised marriage."

"No, nor even mentioned it. Good thing, too, because I don't want to marry you, either."

He made the mistake of leaning back, pillowing his head in his hands and smiling.

Mair briskly picked up his breeches and threw them at him. "Get dressed and get out, Ivor."

"What?" he cried, sitting up again and barely managing to catch his tunic as it flew over his head. "What's the matter?"

She tossed his shirt at him. "Nothing. I want to

be alone tonight, is all, and since we are neither of us interested in marriage, we neither of us owe the other anything, including explanations. So please get dressed and go away.''

He jumped from the bed as she laid hold of his boot and grabbed her arm to stop her from throwing it. ''Mair, I never said anything about marriage. Did you think I had?''

Ignoring his naked body, gazing into his anxious, confused face, she let the boot fall to the floor with a thud. ''No.''

''I never said I loved you—and you've never said you loved me, either.''

''I know.''

He studied her face. ''Do you love me? Is that what's wrong?''

''No, I don't love you.''

''Thank God!'' he sighed. Then he grimaced. ''I'm sorry, Mair.''

He had done nothing so terribly wrong; the trouble was with her. ''No, I'm sorry, Ivor. I still like you, but not tonight. All right?''

''As you say, we don't owe any explanations to each other,'' he said as he tugged on his breeches. ''I'd rather stay, Mair, because I like you and I like being with you, but if you ask me to go, then I'll respect your wishes.''

His softly-spoken words touched her.

Ivor was a good man. He did respect her, certainly far more than Trystan ever would or could. He didn't say one thing, and do another. He never made her feel ashamed for her feelings and desires.

Nevertheless, she knew she could not make love with Ivor tonight.

Two nights later, the baron lay staring at the ceiling of his bedchamber, his equally wide awake wife beside him. "I don't understand him, though he is my son. One minute he's looking like he's about to propose marriage to her, the next he's telling me he's going to Griffydd's."

"Trystan's a young man old enough to be entitled to his secrets. He must have a good reason for going."

The baron sighed and scratched his empty eye socket. "I wish I had your calm, my love. All this mystery is too disturbing. Why do *you* think he went?"

"I would like to believe it could be as simple as wanting to ensure that the wool shipment arrives safely."

"But you don't."

"Unfortunately, no. I suspect our son wanted to take some time to be sure before he makes an important decision."

"And that would be to ask for Lady Rosamunde's hand."

"Yes."

"Maybe he's having doubts, then," the baron proposed hopefully.

"It could be. Yet it is also in Trystan's nature to make decisions cautiously."

"Aye, he's never impetuous, that boy."

"Man, Emryss. Trystan is a man, and I am relieved he doesn't act hastily. We both know that can lead to trouble."

Her husband grinned ruefully. "Abducting you was the smartest thing I ever did."

She briefly returned his smile. "Nevertheless, I am glad Trystan is more sensible."

"If only he had taken Sir Edward with him! That Norman has been pestering me with questions ever since Trystan rode out the gate about where he was going, and why, and the price of wool, and how much Diarmad takes for a fee."

"Perhaps he is curious about the wool trade."

"I hope that's it, but truly, Roanna, I can't stand the man. He's like Mott on the scent. I swear I'm going to tell him to take himself and his questions to the devil."

"Trystan will be home soon," she reminded him. "Keep the conversation to simple pleasantries. It isn't necessary to give Sir Edward any direct answers."

"Easy enough for you to say," Emryss muttered. "You can always claim to have business in the kitchen or the storerooms, or the laundry. I have to entertain the fellow.''

''That does not mean you have to discuss anything specific.''

''But he keeps asking such nosy questions!''

Roanna turned on her side and regarded her husband lovingly. ''You survived after Richard left you behind at Acre, wounded and near death. Can you not survive Sir Edward D'Heureux?''

Her husband scowled, then chuckled softly. ''I suppose I can—although I am beginning to think a Saracen warrior an easier opponent.''

''Do you think he approves of Trystan as a potential suitor to his daughter?''

''Yes, I do, and that's what troubles me most. A Norman like that should be horrified at the prospect of intermingling his family's blood with any taint of Welsh.''

''Perhaps he is more enlightened than you give him credit for.''

The baron sniffed derisively. ''Enlightened? Him? I would sooner believe the king has two heads.'' He shook his own. ''No, there is something amiss with Sir Edward.''

''And his daughter? What do you think of her now?''

''What do *you* think of her, my beloved interrogator? I've noticed you've spent more time with her these past two days than you had to. Surely your opinion should count for more than mine.''

''I am certain she wants to marry Trystan.''

Her husband cursed softly. ''I was afraid you would say that.''

''Unfortunately, I do not know why she wants to.''

''Because Trystan is a fine young man with wonderful parents,'' he supplied in answer. ''What more need we know?''

''I would know exactly why Rosamunde has selected Trystan. If we discover that, perhaps we could prevent a marriage with little harm or bad feelings on either side. The good thing is, Trystan has apparently not spoken of marriage to anybody, not even the lady.''

''You sound certain that she has decided upon him, as if he has no say in the matter. He's our son, Roanna, not some fish to be bought at a market.''

''Of course I agree. Nevertheless, I still think we must be very careful with what we say to Trystan and Rosamunde and her father. Indeed, I would say as little as possible to Sir Edward,'' she cautioned him. ''It could be that Trystan does have reservations, and all our fears will come to naught.''

''If he does decide he wants to marry her, what should we do?''

"Welcome her into our family, of course. Perhaps once she knows she is loved and cherished…"

"You think that is her trouble? I thought it was greed."

"What is greed but a desire to have some worth, in money if nothing else?"

"Once again, my love, my own, I bow to your wisdom."

"Emryss, I don't want my son to marry a woman who doesn't love him, but if he does, I shall have to hope she will someday."

"Since you married out of necessity and came to love your husband, who am I to disagree?"

His wife laughed softly as she nestled against him. "You know very well I was in love with you from the time you first took off your helmet and looked up at me."

Then she sighed mournfully. "Unfortunately, I fear Lady Rosamunde does not feel the same when she looks at Trystan."

Three days later, Trystan rode slowly through the forest on the path that bordered the river as he returned from his brother's castle that lay to the north of Craig Fawr.

If his father thought his sudden desire to go with the wool shipment to Griffydd's unusual, he had said nothing.

As for Lady Rosamunde, Trystan had told her only that he did not welcome being away from her, but would look forward to his return when, he had pledged inwardly, he would be better able to ask for her hand in marriage with a clear mind and willing heart.

Visiting his brother and his family was a welcome change. Seona, Griffydd's wife, was pleasant and thankfully nearly totally recovered from the difficult birth of the twins two years ago. That had almost killed her, and Trystan knew that his wife's death would have nearly killed the strong, reticent Griffydd, too. Now, both seemed more than content to live simply and happily, enjoying their children.

Trystan was more certain than ever that such a quiet life was not for him. He didn't condemn those who were content with what they had; he simply wanted more.

His reverie was interrupted by a sudden cry.

As he abruptly pulled his horse to a halt, a body fell to the ground from one of the tall oaks a few feet in front of him.

Trystan was off his horse in an instant. He ran to the boy, recognizing Arthur almost at once and noting that he had mercifully fallen in a pile of damp leaves and earth instead of the hard dirt of the path. "Are you hurt?"

Brushing himself off and frowning disgruntedly, Arthur got to his feet. "No. I slipped."

Trystan smiled. Dylan couldn't come up with such a scowl in twenty years. "Climbing trees, eh? Nothing broken, I take it."

Arthur gave him a sidelong glance. "You've been away."

It sounded more like an accusation than Trystan would have liked, but he answered genially. "I've been to see Griffydd and Seona. Are you alone, or is Trefor hereabouts, too? Will he come dropping out of the sky like a ripe apple?"

"Trefor is with our father."

"Ah."

Trystan was sure he recognized the cause of Arthur's obvious discontent, besides a few bruises and the embarrassment of slipping from his perch. To Dylan's credit, he didn't seem to play favorites, but it might not look that way to Arthur.

"I've got some sweetmeats in my pack that Seona made. They're really for Lady Roanna, but I don't think she'd mind if you had one," he offered.

The boy shrugged. "I don't mind."

"Good." Trystan went back to his horse and led it off the path, where he tied it to a bush. Then he procured the sweetmeats and went back to Arthur, who had plunked himself down near the path.

Trystan sat beside him and held out the treat. Arthur took it without a word and started to nibble.

"She's a good cook, isn't she?" he asked after a moment.

Arthur nodded. "But not as good as my mam," he mumbled with his mouth full.

Trystan kept a serious expression on his face, for this was a blatant falsehood. Mair was a terrible cook. However, he could admire Arhtur's loyalty.

It seemed Arthur was well aware that Trystan knew he wasn't being exactly truthful, because he blushed. Then he scowled. "That Ivor tells her she's a good cook all the time."

"You sound as if you don't like the captain of the baron's guards."

"I'd like him better if he slept in the barracks."

Trystan struggled to keep his countenance matter-of-fact and changed the subject. "How long is Trefor to stay with Dylan this time?"

"A whole fortnight."

"A whole fortnight, eh? When are you to visit him again?"

"I don't know."

"What does your mother say?"

Arthur shrugged.

"Your father does love you, you know," Trystan said quietly, and sincerely.

"That's what Mam says."

"Don't you believe her?"

Arthur cast a very shrewd and disconcertingly searching glance at his companion. "Then why don't we live with him all the time? Why didn't he marry my mother?"

Trystan wished he had not ventured an opinion at all. "Those questions are for your mother and father to answer, not me."

"You're his foster brother. Don't you know?"

"Have you asked your mother?"

Before Arthur could reply, somebody else did.

Chapter Five

"Has he asked his mother what?"

Trystan scrambled to his feet to face Mair, who had appeared like some sort of spirit on the path. She wore her usual plain garments that nevertheless could not disguise her shapely figure. Today her simple woolen gown was a dark blue like the sky at dusk. The white fabric of her chemise peeked out at the neck, hiding the cleavage of her breasts. Her thick, curling brown hair was drawn back in a braid and a few tendrils escaped to brush her cheeks and forehead.

He had never really noticed the perfect heart shape of her upper lip, or the way she tilted her head back ever so slightly when she was surprised.

"What are you doing here?" he asked. As he spoke, he realized she carried a large, white square of linen over her arm.

Her gaze was slightly hostile as she regarded the

knight. "Not that it's any of your business, Sir Trystan, but I am going to bathe. I came to find Arthur first," she continued, her tone becoming more genial as she turned to look at her son, "to tell him his father has come to see him."

Arthur jumped to his feet. "He has?"

"Yes," Mair said, her eyes sparkling with happiness as she smiled at the delighted Arthur.

Trystan didn't think he'd ever seen her smile that way at anybody else, certainly not him. Nor even Dylan.

He also had the distinct impression he was being deliberately ignored. He should simply turn and walk away, he told himself.

But he did not.

"He has been to see me already to ask if you can go home with him tomorrow," she said to her son. "He thinks you should stay a little more than a fortnight."

"More than a fortnight?" Arthur repeated with happy wonder, a happiness that Trystan couldn't help sharing, given their conversation moments ago.

"That is what he said," Mair confirmed as, still ignoring Trystan, she came toward her son and put her arm around his shoulder.

"Oh, can I?" Arthur cried.

"Of course. Your things are already packed. We are to dine in the great hall tonight, and you will stay the night there and leave with your father in the morning. Now off with you, because he's anxious to see you, too.''

Arthur needed no further urging. In an instant, he had disappeared from view and only the sound of his young feet pounding along the path told them he ever had been there.

Mair watched him go, then seemed to recall that Trystan was nearby. He almost wished she hadn't as she ran her impertinent gaze over him. "I see you have returned to Craig Fawr, too."

"Obviously," he replied. "And Dylan here, as well. My parents will be pleased."

She smiled slyly. "Not so much as Lady Rosamunde to see you, perhaps. I hear she has been mooning about like a dazed calf during your absence."

"Who told you that? Ivor?"

Her smug smile dissipated. "It is common gossip." She turned toward the river. "Good day."

"You're not really going to bathe here by yourself?"

She paused, glancing back at him with that mischievous, elfin grin lighting her features. "Do you want to join me?"

He frowned darkly. "That is not what I meant. It is not safe for you to do that alone, and besides, the water must be freezing."

"I like to bathe in the cold water. And I do not need a guard, so again, sir, I give you good day."

With an insolent toss of her chestnut braid, she started forward, pushing through some low bushes that grew close to the riverbank.

"Mair, although this wood is generally safe, a lone woman may be too tempting for any brigands passing through," he said as he hurried after her.

Especially a lone woman who looks as pretty as you, he added inwardly.

Then he chided himself for the observation, and began to wonder if five days had really been long enough to get over his foolish lust for her.

By the time he reached her, she had already undone her thick braid, so that her bountiful hair fell around her shoulders and breasts. His breath caught at the sight of it and he had a sudden, strong desire to bury his hands in it.

He reminded himself of Lady Rosamunde's blond hair, hair that was always covered by a cap and a scarf of such fine and costly fabric, a man could fear he would inadvertently tear it if he touched it.

"Mair," he said as firmly as he could, "we have to talk."

"I have already told you I have no intention of telling anyone about what we did, so there is nothing more to talk about between us, I don't think."

"It's Arthur."

Her expression grew defiant. "What of my son?"

"He wanted to know why you don't live with Dylan and why Dylan didn't marry you."

Her steadfast gaze faltered. "What did you reply?" she asked softly, and with obvious uncertainty.

Trystan felt as if one of the stones from the castle wall had suddenly dropped on his head. He had never in his life imagined that Mair worried about anything, or had a single doubt in her lively head. "That he should ask that question of you and Dylan," he finally replied. "I thought you should be prepared."

She sighed. "I shall have to pray for divine guidance when he does, I fear," she said as if to herself.

Then she raised her eyes to regard Trystan with her usual bold, steadfast gaze. "I thank you for the warning. Now if you will excuse me, the time grows short. Unlike some people who can do what they like when they like, I have much to do."

"Let him ask Dylan his questions," he suggested gently.

Mair frowned and a flash of defiance brightened her brown eyes flecked with gold. "I will not. He is my son, and I owe it to him to try to explain that not everyone who makes love gets married, and that you don't need to be married to make a baby."

Suddenly, another stone seemed to fall on his

head. God's wounds, it could be that he had given Mair a child, too!

His child. And Mair's child.

How could he not have considered this possibility before?

He knew how—he had been too busy condemning himself for his lust and dreaming about marrying Rosamunde.

Anwyl, he should be horrified, not thinking of this eventuality with such…delight. And pride.

God save him, he was already imagining how the infant would look.

"Had you not better hurry on to the castle?" Mair asked. "Lady Rosamunde will likely be patroling the wall walk waiting for you." Her expression altered to one of concern. "What is it? Are you ill?"

"No, no," he said, brushing his hair from his forehead as if that could help him think. "I just…I have to go."

"So go then."

"I will."

With that, he turned and made his way back through the bushes, pausing to steady himself against a tree as another realization assailed him, one that did destroy the happiness that the idea of fathering Mair's child produced.

As he had told Mair before, he had plans. Ambitious plans. Plans that would finally make him important in his own right, and for those to be fulfilled, he needed to marry a woman like Lady Rosamunde.

No, no, he wanted to marry Lady Rosamunde, who also had beauty to recommend her.

Surely she would not look with favor on a bridegroom who had sired a child even as he was courting her.

Wheeling around, he marched back to the riverbank—to discover that a naked Mair was only waist-deep in the frigid water.

Equally surprised, she turned around, making no move at all to cover herself.

Despite their lovemaking, he had never seen her naked body and although he could not see all of her, he saw enough to render him immobile.

Her unbound hair brushed her magnificent breasts, their nipples puckered with the cold. Her skin was flawless, her form like that of a goddess. Her lips were half open as if in desire, her eyes wide and without that shrewd expression that made him think she found him amusing, as she might a child.

He swallowed hard as she continued to face him without a hint of modesty. "What do you want now?" she demanded.

He felt as if he were in some kind of daze. "I...I cannot speak to you like that."

"Then go away and we will speak later tonight in the hall, if we must."

"No!" He couldn't do that. He couldn't talk to Mair when Lady Rosamunde would be nearby. "It has to be now."

"You may be a knight and destined to be a lord one day, Sir Trystan DeLanyea," Mair replied with a disgruntled frown, "but you do not, and never will, have command over *me*."

With that, she turned away and dived into the deeper part of the river, the motion revealing her pale buttocks and long, slim legs.

Trystan sat heavily on the bank, then buried his head in his folded arms. He had to make her understand that he could not acknowledge any child she bore eight or nine months hence as his.

Yet to deny his own child...

He had to do it. It was too important that he achieve his goal. Besides, if he did acknowledge the child, and Lady Rosamunde refused to marry him because of that, might he not come to hate the child who had thwarted his success? Better to deny the child to prevent that, for its own sake.

And how could he even be sure any child of Mair's was his? It was no secret that she gave her favors freely. Hadn't Arthur's disparaging remarks proved that Ivor came to Mair's bed?

He did not begrudge Ivor that. No, he did not, especially now, when he could always put the credit—no, the blame—onto the captain of the guard's shoulders.

He heard water splashing and glanced up to see Mair dash from the river and grab the linen square. She was as fleet of foot as a deer, yet not so fast that he didn't see more of her perfect body before, panting and blue-lipped, she wrapped herself in the linen.

"You really must think what you have to say important," she noted as her teeth started to chatter.

He rose. "I told you the river would be freezing."

"And I told you I like it that way," she retorted as she began to rub herself. "Now, what do you want to say?"

"If you find you are with child soon, I will never claim it."

Mair let the linen fall to the ground and began to dress with swift, brisk movements.

"I am going to ask Lady Rosamunde to marry me," he continued, "and I won't have anything interfere with that. As you said, we are both responsible for our mistake. Besides, any child you bear after this could be Ivor's, too, or some other man's, for all I know."

Mair reached down to retrieve the damp linen. When she straightened, her face was inscrutable as she regarded him. "If I am with child, would you have me leave Craig Fawr to spare your bride the knowledge that you lusted after another?"

"Yes."

"Would you pay to make it so?" she asked with shocking coolness.

He stared at her, dumbfounded. He had never, ever, thought Mair the least bit greedy.

"Would you be willing to pay money for me to take what could be your child far away," Mair went on inexorably, "so that the Norman lady you want to marry doesn't discover you were loving another woman while you were courting her?"

"Mair," he began, upset at the dishonorable connotation of her words—a connotation he could not, in all conscience, deny. What was she saying but the truth? Nevertheless, he had his plans to consider. "If you would be willing—"

Before he could say more, she strode up to him and slapped him hard across the face. "If I am ashamed of anything," she said between clenched teeth, "it is that I didn't do that the moment I met you on the wall walk. I am ashamed that I let a man who would rather pay money than acknowledge his own child near me."

She took a step closer, until she was nose to nose with him. "Know you this, Sir Trystan DeLanyea, if I am with child and that child proves to be the very image of you, I would rather die than admit I let you touch me."

She stepped back, an expression of utter scorn on her face. "So rest assured, Lady Rosamunde need never know your secret. And may you be happy with the wife you deserve!'' she snapped as she marched past him.

"Time for young warriors to be abed, I am thinking," Dylan DeLanyea said to Arthur in the crowded great hall of Craig Fawr that night. The younger baron's dark eyes were as merry as his smile as he deftly prevented the boy from protesting. "We have an early start in the morning, my son, so no use looking at me like that. Kiss your mam good night and farewell, and off you go."

Mair leaned her cheek toward the boy, who pecked her as a chicken might a piece of grain. "Be a good boy for your father and Lady Genevieve, Arthur, and do as they ask. Then hurry home. I miss your noise when you're not here."

Arthur flushed, and she knew he found even this slight hint of maternal love rather much to bear when they were in company. "I will. Good night, Mam."

"Good night, Arthur."

Mair kept her gaze on her son's back as he made his way through the hall toward the tower stairs leading to Dylan's room. There he would spend the night, and in the morning, he would be gone for two long weeks.

Mair meant what she said. She missed Arthur's noise, which he and she both knew meant his company. She had a hearty dislike of being alone.

And she would much rather ignore the sight of Trystan and Lady Rosamunde seated together at the high table and whispering like lovers. Trystan looked nearly as handsome as dark-haired Dylan in his black tunic trimmed with gold, while the lady looked as lovely as a vision, with a green gown of some kind of fabric that shimmered in the torch light. Her many jewels shone, too, and her beauty seemed as ethereal as an angel's. Tonight, even her smile looked luminous.

Perhaps Trystan had already asked her to be his bride and she had accepted.

Mair hoped they both got warts.

"He's growing to be a fine lad, isn't he?" Dylan declared proudly.

With a warm smile, Mair turned to the handsome warrior. She had always liked Dylan, who was bold and honest and passionate. He was truly a good-looking fellow. Even tonight, dressed in the same simple clothes he had worn since his arrival, he looked better than many a man in the finest garments money could buy. Of course, it was not only due to the excellence of his body; there was a natural, pleasant charm to Dylan that no amount of study could achieve, or coins purchase. "I think it must be my excellent cooking."

Dylan laughed, the low, joyous rumble making all around them smile, too.

Indeed, if there was one fault with Dylan, it was

that he too much enjoyed being the center of regard. "I think it must be in spite of that."

The rest of the folk at the table made murmurs of protest, while exchanging amused glances as they waited for Mair to answer. "You never tasted my *food,*" she replied evenly.

Their tablemates chuckled.

"Tell me you are not raising my son on ale."

"Everybody drinks ale," Mair replied, "and mine's the best, but he eats enough to feed a foot patrol, too."

"I will warn my wife to make extra, then."

Mair laughed softly, regarding her former lover amiably. "An excellent idea."

As the maidservants arrived to clear the table, a minstrel struck up a tune. Just as quickly, the men, including Dylan, all rose to push the tables against the wall to clear the floor for dancing. Several people hurried out onto the central space, including the baron and his wife.

"Are you in a mood to dance?" Dylan asked as he joined her on a bench.

"No, not even with you. With all the company the baron's been having, I've been busy in the brewery. I thought having Normans wouldn't be so bad, but that Sir Edward likes my ale."

"As well he should. What of your *braggot?* That's nectar for the gods."

Mair grinned. "Wanting the poor man to have

a head in the morning, are you? Too strong for Normans, that. They think that because it tastes like spicy mead, it's no more harmful than that. They forget it's got ale to it, too."

"Aye, and I know about the head the next day," Dylan admitted ruefully. "An ache that makes torture sound like a blessed relief. Look you, I think he's gone through a cask of ale already," he continued, nodding at Sir Edward, who sat beside the baron with an expression of sodden, beatific calm.

Dylan looked at the couple beside Sir Edward at the high table. "So, when are they announcing the betrothal?"

"Who?" she asked, following his gaze.

"Why, Trystan and that Lady Rosamunde."

Mair smiled to hear the echo of her son's scorn for "that Ivor" in his father's voice. "You don't sound as if you approve. She's very beautiful."

"*Anwyl,* Mair, I got eyes."

Mair gave him a knowing, sidelong glance. "Isn't that enough?"

"No," he replied with sudden seriousness. Then he grinned again, because Dylan was rarely serious for long. "She may be all right enough, but she looks as stiff as an icicle and about as warm. I'd like to think Trystan had more sense than to marry for beauty or wealth or power."

"Truly, my lord?" Mair said with feigned innonocence. "Is that not what persuaded you to marry at last?"

He gave her a mildly sour look. "No, and you know it. Mind, I wouldn't throw such things on a dung heap."

"Neither would Trystan."

She wished she had kept any trace of annoyance from her voice as Dylan looked at her quizzically. "As you said, a man shouldn't throw such things on a dung heap," she said lightly.

"For a moment, I thought you were jealous."

"Of that woman?" Mair scoffed with a laugh. "To be sure, I like her clothes, but they'd hardly do for wearing in the brewery, would they? Or are you thinking I am jealous of your wife? *Anwyl,* Dylan, not for an instant," she answered truthfully, the knowledge of just how much that was true suddenly striking her.

And she wasn't going to be jealous of Trystan's wife, either.

"Maybe I've had too much wine," Dylan noted meditatively as he glanced down at his goblet.

Mair realized they were as alone as they were likely to get in the hall and took a deep breath. "I think I should warn you, Dylan, that Arthur may ask you why we don't live with you, and why you didn't marry me."

"Ah!" Dylan sighed.

"What will you tell him?"

"What did you say?"

"He hasn't asked me yet."

"Then what makes you think to warn me now, and so gravely, too?"

"Trystan was talking to him today, and I gather he asked Trystan."

"Trystan?" Dylan asked, his eyes widening.

"I was as surprised as you to hear of it."

"Trystan told you of Arthur's question?"

"Yes."

Dylan frowned and looked as displeased as it was possible for him to look. "What answer did he give?"

"That Arthur should ask us."

"Thanks be to God for that!" Dylan said sincerely. "I can just imagine what other explanation Trystan might have given if he had been in one of his I-am-the-most-honorable-man-in-Britain moods. Too much of the Norman in my foster brother, I think."

"What will you tell Arthur?" Mair persisted, turning the conversation away from her meeting with Trystan and back to the more important matter at hand.

"I will explain that you don't live with me because you have always lived here and this is your home," he said. "And we didn't marry because...because...."

"Because you are a lord and I am an alewife?"

"*Anwyl*, Mair," Dylan muttered, running a hand over his chin, "that sounds terrible."

"It's partly true. Or you could say I wouldn't

marry you because you are a lord, and I am not a lady.''

''That is not an improvement, and he might feel himself inferior if I say that, although he is my son.''

''He knows full well he is your *younger* son,'' she said. ''He sometimes thinks you prefer Trefor to him, and Trefor plays upon that fear.''

''I know,'' Dylan replied gravely. ''There's good and bad in the DeLanyea tree, and sometimes I fear Trefor's got some of that bad. I'll do my best to weed it out, and to make certain Arthur knows I love my sons the same, as I would love other children, too, if I had them.''

''Has Genevieve…?'' Mair asked, her heart filling with both sympathy and empathy for Dylan's wife as he slowly shook his head.

''If Arthur didn't question you, maybe he won't question me,'' Dylan said after a moment.

Mair had to smile. Dylan saw the sun behind every cloud. ''You could tell him it's because I wasn't pretty enough.''

''Mair!''

''You could tell him you were the most fickle man in the castle and I would have laughed in your face if you'd been mad enough to ask me.''

''Now you're wounding my tender feelings. I have been absolutely faithful to my wife and I have no intention of ever being unfaithful,'' he replied firmly. He glanced at the dancers and grew serious again. "Unfortunately, I doubt the young lady dancing with our Trystan would share that sentiment."

Mair followed his gaze toward Lady Rosamunde, who was moving as gracefully as a willow bending in the breeze.

"Oh, she's subtle, that one," Dylan said softly, "but as sure as I know women, she'll never be happy in one man's bed."

Although Mair told herself she didn't care about Trystan's future wife and her faithfulness or lack thereof, Mair felt ill nonetheless. "You think she will take lovers?"

Dylan turned to her with a sardonic smile. "I would be willing to bet a considerable sum that I could get her into my bed tonight, if I were so inclined."

Mair regarded him incredulously. "How can you be so sure?"

"Do you doubt my expertise?" he queried.

As Dylan had said, he did know women. Not as well as he seemed to think, perhaps, but she could not ignore his concern. "Are you going to tell Trystan what you think?"

"I believe I would do better to speak to the baron. Trystan would only get angry and say that I am hardly in a position to be preaching about fidelity, given my history before my marriage."

"But you never had more than one lover at a time, and you weren't married. Nor was there ever talk of marriage, or even love, I don't think,'' Mair said. ''I know he's a prig, but surely he can't compare the two.''

''You know Trystan,'' Dylan replied wryly. ''He can and he probably will.'' He grinned his irrepressible grin. ''Well, let us hope Trystan doesn't ask for her. Now, speaking of marriage, how's Ivor?''

Mair tried not to look annoyed at his assumption. ''I have no marriage plans, and neither does Ivor. And I would not mention Ivor when you are with Arthur. Arthur doesn't like him.''

''There's a nick in the arrow tip, eh?''

Mair shrugged.

''Very well, I shall not mention Ivor,'' Dylan said with a chuckle. ''It will be enough that I may have to explain why I didn't marry you.''

Mair regarded him steadily. ''Just tell Arthur the truth, Dylan. Tell him you didn't love me enough to ask, and I didn't love you enough that I would have accepted you if you had.''

Chapter Six

Lady Rosamunde danced perfectly, too. Trystan enjoyed watching her graceful, expert motions as they circled the floor in a round dance, and wondered how he could have forgotten that during his brief absence. Even now, he could tell he was the envy of several of the men in the hall, and this was only a dance.

Indeed, what young man could keep his gaze from such womanly perfection?

Oddly enough, it seemed Dylan—who had found women an object of fascination nearly from birth—was well able to, for he hardly glanced at Lady Rosamunde. Perhaps whatever he was discussing so earnestly with Mair was more important. They were probably talking about Arthur.

Not that it mattered to Trystan what they were talking about. Mair had said she would not reveal their…indiscretion…and he didn't doubt that she was a woman of her word.

Nor did he doubt that Dylan was being anything more than a friend to his former lover. Dylan truly loved his wife, and would continue to be faithful to her.

The dance ended and Trystan escorted Lady Rosamunde back to her cushioned chair on the dais. As he did so, he signaled for Gwen to bring them some wine.

Gwen didn't look pleased to do so, but at least she did it, and Trystan commanded himself to pay attention to Lady Rosamunde rather than a disgruntled servant.

Fanning herself gracefully with her slender hand, Lady Rosamunde surveyed the gathering in the hall. "Who is that old fellow your father is listening to with such interest? A merchant? If so, I fear his business must not be good, for he is very poorly dressed."

Following her gaze, Trystan said, "That is Aneirin, the most senior and respected of my father's shepherds."

Lady Rosamunde's rosy lips frowned. "He is a shepherd?" she asked incredulously.

"Aneirin has forgotten more about sheep than most men ever know," Trystan explained with a smile. "My father relies on his advice a great deal."

"Oh." Lady Rosamunde took a delicate sip of her wine and again her blue-eyed gaze perused the hall. "Who is that speaking with your cousin?"

"Her name is Mair," Trystan replied nonchalantly. "She makes the ale your father likes so much."

Trystan was surprised to see Lady Rosamunde's nose wrinkle with distaste, then recalled that Normans generally favored wine. Ale was something for the Saxons and other peasants to drink. "It is very good ale," he offered. "It is a pity he had to retire before the dancing."

"Yes, but he has experienced this malady before, and I assure you, it is nothing serious."

Trystan nodded, thankful that Sir Edward's illness must be minor. Otherwise, his daughter would be more concerned.

He remembered the time Arthur and Trefor had eaten too many green apples. Mair had been beside herself until she discovered the cause of their pains. To be sure, she had not completely relaxed until their stomachaches had ceased and it was evident they were completely recovered, but surely he couldn't judge every woman by Mair. Mair loved her son dearly.

Well, surely Lady Rosamunde loved her father just as well.

"Why would your cousin, a baron, speak with such a wench?" Lady Rosamunde asked, interrupting his reverie. "Why is she allowed in this hall, as if she were…" She hesitated, a tiny wrinkle marring her brow. "As if she were important."

"She is the mother of Dylan's younger son."

"Ah, she is the one. She looks so…common."

Trystan's jaw tightened. "You know about Dylan's children?"

Lady Rosamunde flushed and smiled bashfully. "I have made it my business to find out about your family. I…I hope you are not offended."

"Offended? No," he said, his momentary flash of anger appeased by her embarrassment, "but I am curious to know why."

And curious to know if she had heard of his desire for his cousin's wife, a desire that had lasted until Genevieve had shown him the futility of his youthful infatuation.

He was free of that boyish passion now, so only his persistent lust for Mair gave him any concern. And the way he felt in her arms after they had coupled, the perfect peace as if he had arrived where he truly belonged, must be his mind's attempts to ease a guilty conscience.

Lady Rosamunde's blush deepened. She glanced at him, then away. "You should not ask a lady why she does a thing," she said softly.

This was how a woman should behave, with modesty and humility and shyness.

"You should not judge the DeLanyeas by Dylan's behavior," he said.

Lady Rosamunde's eyes widened. "Oh, I understand it is men's natures to...to do such things."

"*Some* men's natures," Trystan corrected.

Lady Rosamunde's smile was glorious to behold. "And I hear he has been faithful to his wife ever since they married." She glanced at Dylan and Mair. "At least as far as anyone knows."

Her sly tone took him aback. "I assure you, he has been faithful. He loves his wife very much, and she loves him."

"I am glad to hear it," Lady Rosamunde replied. "But of course, if a vintner samples other wine, that is to be expected, too, and a wise woman accepts it."

Trystan's brow furrowed. Was she saying that she would overlook a husband's infidelity? Did she think that would please him?

Did she want to please him so much, she would say even that? How much more evidence did he require of her willingness to accept him? Surely he need not hesitate to ask for her hand.

"Lady Rosamunde D'Heureux, truly words cannot do justice to your beauty," Dylan declared from somewhere close by.

Trystan tried not to scowl as his boisterous cousin sauntered toward them.

Dylan put a mournful frown on his darkly handsome face, yet the expression in his eyes remained unabashedly merry. "I have been waiting to speak with you at some moment when Trystan was not monopolizing your company, but I am beginning to fear that will not happen tonight. Since I must leave on the morrow, I hope you will forgive me for interrupting."

Trystan was not willing to forgive Dylan for anything, and certainly not for smiling at Lady Rosamunde as if she were…any woman.

"I cannot mind when you interrupt to pay me a compliment, Baron DeLanyea," Lady Rosamunde murmured.

Trystan knew she didn't mean to point out the difference in rank between them. Dylan's father had been a baron, and Dylan inherited the title, even though he was illegitimate. Trystan's father had paid to ensure that under a system established to accommodate Norman law and Welsh tradition—and incidentally add to the Norman king's coffers.

Without waiting for any further invitation, Dylan sat, insinuating himself between Trystan and Lady Rosamunde. "I am sorry I was unable to converse with your father. I trust his illness is not serious?"

"Oh, no, a small malady of the stomach. He has suffered from it before."

"I am glad it is minor. How are you finding Wales?"

"Delightful, and your uncle is a wonderful host."

As his charming, courteous cousin continued to engage Lady Rosamunde in conversation, Trystan stopped trying to hide his scowl. Just when he was about to ask Lady Rosamunde for her hand, Dylan had to interrupt.

Maybe he should have guessed Dylan would do that sooner rather than later. Even happily married, Dylan could no more prevent himself from speaking to a beautiful woman than he could cease to breathe.

At the sound of Lady Rosamunde's delicate laugh, Trystan glanced at her. She was flushed and smiling, and obviously finding Dylan's conversation most pleasant.

Damn his cousin. Couldn't he be content with winning the love of his wife? Couldn't he be happy having captured the affection of so many women—aye, and retaining that affection, too, even after he had broken off with them? Wasn't it enough that he could still talk amiably to Mair and genially discuss their child, and smile at her and have her smile back in that frank, approving way that started in the depths of her brown eyes and spread over her vivacious face?

Trystan rose abruptly. "If you will both excuse me, I think I need some fresher air."

He marched from the hall, paying no heed to anyone's curious glances. Nor did he pause and look back. He strode across the courtyard and up to the wall walk. Once there, he took great, deep breaths of the cool, clear air as he surveyed the countryside and nearby hills.

"*Anwyl*, running a race, are we?"

He spun around and saw Dylan grinning in the moonlight. "What are you doing here?"

"Wanting to talk with you, boy, is all. No need to look like you'd like to toss me over the edge."

"I am not a boy."

"No, no, you're not. Lady Rosamunde doesn't look to think so, either. Are you planning to wed her?"

"It is no business of yours if I am."

"Of course it is. Your marriage means an alliance of my family with another, so it must concern me."

Trystan could not argue with this; however, he had no wish to share his plans with anybody yet, Dylan most of all. "Perhaps I am. Would you object?"

"Is there a reason I should?"

"I don't think so."

"What does your father say?"

"He hasn't spoken against it."

"I see." Dylan strolled over to the merlon and leaned back against it. "Then neither shall I."

"How wonderful to have your permission," Trystan replied sarcastically.

"You should be glad I don't disapprove."

"Who could find fault with Lady Rosamunde? You seemed to find her pleasant enough to speak to."

"Jealous?"

"Not of you."

"I am glad to hear you say that. Otherwise, I would have to kill you for the insult to my honor that would imply. When are you going to ask her?"

Trystan answered slowly and distinctly. "In my own good time."

"Is Mair quite well?"

His question startled Trystan and he felt a sharp stab like a dagger point in his flesh at the notion that she might be ill. "What makes you ask that?"

Dylan shrugged. "She looked a little pale and more worried than I like."

"I think she's concerned about Arthur," Trystan offered in explanation, telling himself that had to be all.

He had never known Mair to be seriously ill. Indeed, he couldn't even imagine that.

Why, if anything happened to her, he would be…and Arthur…

He was getting carried away. Mair hadn't been ill the last time he had seen her. "You should be thinking about what you're going to say to Arthur. He asked me—"

"Ah, yes, my inquisitive son and his questions to come. She told me what you said to him," Dylan said gravely. "I thank you for suggesting he come to us with his questions."

"How could I do otherwise? I didn't have the answer."

"Mair says I should tell him that I didn't love her enough to ask for her hand and even if I had, she didn't love me enough to accept."

"Truly?" Too late Trystan realized he had blurted out a response. "I am surprised she would admit that to anybody," he continued, trying to sound nonchalant.

"You know our Mair is an honest woman."

"She is not *my* Mair!"

"A slip of the tongue, boy."

"Don't call me 'boy'!"

"I'll try to remember." Dylan grinned slyly. "I visited with Angharad this afternoon."

"So that's what made you think of Mair and me? Is she still standing by her ridiculous prediction that we are going to marry?"

"Actually, she never mentioned Mair at all."

"Good!"

"*Anwyl,* you *are* in a foul mood! I am going to leave you until you are more pleasant."

"I never asked you to join me in the first place."

"Either here or in the hall, eh?" Dylan shoved himself from the wall. "The lady didn't seem to mind."

"What did you expect her to do?"

"Exactly what she did," Dylan replied as he headed for the stairs leading below to the courtyard.

"Angharad didn't speak of Mair," he called back in a teasing tone Trystan was all too familiar with, "but she told me she has dreamed about your children."

"What of children?" Trystan demanded, taking a step after him.

Then he halted and told himself to pay no heed to what was probably a jest.

"They will all be healthy, and have dark hair." Dylan started to disappear down the stairs. "And freckles!"

Trystan's first urge was to run after his cousin and shove him down the stone steps.

Instead, he only scowled deeper before slowly heading in the same direction.

Angharad's predictions were all lies. To be sure, a few came to pass, but why not? He could make predictions, too. The winter would be colder than the autumn. This year, hunting would be good, because the spring had been mild. Because the spring had been mild, the sheeps' coats of wool were not as thick, so his father would not make so much money from the sale of it, and they would not have as much French wine this winter.

As Trystan approached the hall, he heard a noise and halted abruptly, wondering what it was. Then he slowly walked back to the shadowed alley between the hall and the kitchen.

"Ivor?" he demanded of the tall, dark-haired man and a woman standing close together in the darkness.

The captain of the guard swiftly turned. "Yes, sir?"

Trystan saw Mair behind him and a rage such as he had never known engulfed him. "If you want to rut, do it when you are not supposed to be on duty!"

"I'm off duty, sir," Ivor protested.

Strangely, Mair remained silent. No doubt because she had been caught behaving no better than a whore in an alley, he thought.

"Then take your woman to your quarters. The courtyard of my father's castle is not a brothel!"

With that, he turned and marched away.

"I am not a whore!" Mair called out. She felt as if a bolt of lightning had struck her, energizing her from the top of her head to the tips of her toes. "I am a woman, not a cold, lifeless statue! I am good enough to be the mother of your cousin's child!''

Trystan hesitated for a moment, then continued on his way.

''Mair, come—''

Mair ignored Ivor's plea.

''Come back here and face me, you *gnaf!* You faced me before, remember? *Remember?*''

''What the devil are you doing?'' Ivor growled as he hurried after her and pulled her to a halt. ''And him the son of the baron?''

At first, Mair looked at Ivor as if she didn't know who he was. Then she tossed her head and straightened her shoulders defiantly. ''That *gnaf* treated me like a whore.''

''He's right, you know.''

''What are you saying?'' Mair demanded, her voice as stern as any warrior whose honor has been called into question.

''We should be in my quarters, or your house and—''

''You are not upset that he has so little respect for me?''

''He is the baron's son—''

''So he can insult me with impunity?'' Mair's eyes narrowed. ''Or is it that you think your lover is a whore?''

Ivor took hold of her shoulders. ''Mair, please! You know—''

She twisted away from him and faced him angrily. "I know you wouldn't speak up for me when a man insulted me, and that is all I need to know. It is over between us, Ivor."

"Mair!"

"Good night!"

She strode through the courtyard, out the gate and toward her house, cursing Trystan, Ivor and men in general all the way. She was not a whore, and no man could make her believe otherwise.

When Trystan reached the hall, he was still angry, and especially too angry to speak to Lady Rosamunde of marriage. Besides, as he noted almost at once, she was no longer there.

God's wounds, he had been a fool to let Dylan upset him so much! But he was not a fool to chastise Ivor and Mair for behaving as they were in the courtyard. Why, anybody could discover them there. At least on the wall walk, one need only fear the sentry—

The memory of Mair's passion came to him. How freely she gave herself! How fully and fervently—not as if a kiss were a great honor she was bestowing on an unworthy supplicant.

What in the name of the saints was wrong with him? He had been equally wrong to make love with Mair in that place. Or any place.

He pushed all thoughts of Mair and her lover

aside as he put a smile on his face and sat beside his mother.

She did not need to know of the captain of the guard's impropriety.

"Lady Rosamunde has retired?" he asked Lady Roanna.

"Yes. Naturally she wanted to ensure that her father was feeling better before she went to bed." His mother's gaze grew more searching. "You left rather abruptly."

"I hope she wasn't upset. I...I needed some air."

"Oh, are you not feeling well?"

For an instant, Trystan was tempted to say he was not. Indeed, he seemed to be bedeviled by feelings he could not control. "I am perfectly healthy."

"Lady Rosamunde didn't seem upset," his mother assured him.

"Good." Trystan decided now was as good a time as any to tell his mother of his hopes. "I am going to ask her to be my wife."

His mother barely batted an eye, but then she was not given to emotional display. "You love her?"

"Of course, if she is to be my wife."

"And she loves you?"

"I think so. I believe so. Yes."

"I see."

"Do you approve? Will my father? You must, and so must he, for she comes from a fine family, rich and powerful, and she is sweet and beautiful, too."

"If you love this woman, and she loves you, that is all that matters to us."

Trystan knew he should be happy. He *was* happy. Of course, he would be happier when Lady Rosamunde agreed.

"You have not asked her yet?"

"I shall tomorrow."

"It might be better to wait until her father is recovered."

"I understand it is not a serious illness, and one he has had before."

"That is good, but still, Trystan, I think your father would prefer that you wait. We would do well to avoid anything that may cause trouble later."

"How could a minor illness cause trouble later?"

"No alliance between a baron's son and a Norman knight's daughter is going to pass without remark at court, and elsewhere. If Sir Edward gives his approval and agrees to terms, then later hears criticism of his agreement, he could claim he was ill and we took advantage of his weakness."

His father had always claimed his mother was

the wiser of the couple; Trystan had more proof now, if he had ever doubted it. "I understand."

Lady Roanna rose with her usual fluid grace. "I had best drag your father away before they all start singing, or he will be exhausted come the morning." She smiled. "I cannot seem to convince him he is not twenty anymore."

Her gaze softened as she regarded Trystan. "Sleep well, my son, and I hope you will be happy with your choice."

He returned her smile. He had crossed a fence telling his mother of his hope; he would not look back.

And she would tell his father, sparing him—

What? He was not ashamed of his choice in any way. His father would probably make a joke, that's all, or say something to destroy the gravity of his decision, and he didn't want that.

"Any better, Father?" Rosamunde asked as she regarded Sir Edward, who lay in the large wooden bed in the pleasant tower chamber the one-eyed baron had given over to his use while at Craig Fawr.

Besides being furnished with a fine bed adorned with many soft coverings, there was a delicately carved chair. Two fine candles lit the room, casting their bronze glow on her father's red cheeks.

Despite her apparently solicitous question,

Rosamunde knew there was nothing wrong with her father that more courage and a little abstinence from ale wouldn't cure.

"I am a little better. Did he ask you?"

Rosamunde turned away to pour her father a draft of the foul-tasting medicine she had prepared for his particular malady. It didn't cure his headache and stomach quickly, but it would eventually. "Not yet. Soon. His cousin interrupted at a most inopportune time."

"That would be the young baron?"

"Yes." She sighed, thinking it a pity Genevieve Perronet had already captured the handsome young baron before she had a chance. Dylan DeLanyea had the better title and already possessed an estate.

Nevertheless, his many dalliances were legendary, and she wanted a husband who would be so enamored of her, he would do as she willed, at least at first. After a time, of course, a man's ardor would fade, but by then, Rosamunde vowed, she would control the family purse.

Recalling Trystan's petulant departure, she made a little frown. To be sure, his reaction had obviously been caused by his cousin's arrival. Still, Rosamunde had not lingered in the hall after Trystan had marched out. She would not have her future husband think she would wait upon his moods or humors.

He must be influenced by hers.

"You will be better in the morning, Father," she said as she handed him the draught.

"How can I know?" he grumbled before he swiftly downed the bad-tasting mixture.

Her cool, steadfast gaze did not alter. "You will be better in the morning, and ready to receive Trystan DeLanyea's request for my hand in marriage. You will tell him you must think upon it a time."

"What is there to think about if it is as you say with these Welshmen? If he will pay to wed you, why delay? Maybe that will only give him time to reconsider."

"Because we must not seem too eager, or they might get suspicious," Rosamunde explained as if to a child. Then her lips turned up in a confident little smile. "Trust me, Father. He will not reconsider."

Chapter Seven

The next morning, Trystan waited in the small stone chapel of Craig Fawr for mass to begin. The building smelled of stale incense, and the early morning light brought no warmth to its cool interior. As he shifted his feet as much to try to warm himself as to ease his impatience, Trystan could easily imagine that the catacombs of Rome were much like this.

At least he wasn't here for a burial.

As he continued to wait, he wondered if Lady Rosamunde would come, or if her father's illness would necessitate her remaining with him.

In spite of his mother's assurances, he hoped she was not angry with him after last night.

Then he watched with relief as the lovely lady entered the chapel for mass with her father.

As always, she looked placidly beautiful. But there was something...

She was dressed in a splendid gown of scarlet brocade trimmed with ermine that was nearly the same hue as Mair's silk gown. Unfortunately, that color seemed to make Rosamunde's pale complexion look as she lacked a drop of blood in her body, whereas brilliant red apparently suited Mair's darker hair and brown eyes to perfection. Or perhaps it was merely that such a bold color seemed more akin to her personality.

A personality that was frustating and annoying and altogether too rude.

He flushed when Lady Rosamunde looked at him, half fearing she could read his thoughts. He relaxed when she smiled at him. If she were annoyed by his sudden departure last night, she would not look at him thus.

Nevertheless, he thought he would do well not to repeat such childish behavior, no matter what Dylan or anybody else did, just as he must stop thinking about Mair.

He forced his attention to Sir Edward. The older man still did not look completely recovered, yet surely if he were well enough to attend mass, he was well enough to deal with a request for his daughter's hand.

Provided Lady Rosamunde accepted him first, of course.

But she must. All last night, Trystan had told

himself this and tried to think of anything she might conceivably hold against him.

He was not a lord or a baron—yet. If he worked hard and pleased the king or one of the powerful nobles at court, however, such a reward was attainable, especially given the reputation of his family.

He was not as rich a husband as a woman of her caliber could hope for, but again, he was young. There was time for him to earn a fortune of his own.

He could think of no criticism she had made of him personally, either to his face, or to anybody else. To be sure, he was not as unremittingly merry as Dylan—but that was good. Nor was he so grim as Griffydd, whose laughter was so rare, it elicited comment if he so much as chuckled.

Despite these comforting ruminations, Trystan was not so arrogant that he didn't suppose there was something worthy of criticism about him, and so he had spent the night in an agony of worry.

And an agony of lust.

But not for Lady Rosamunde.

For Mair. He kept thinking about being in her arms again, surrendering himself to the unbridled passion she inspired, as well as her unrestrained response. God's wounds, how she loved—as boldly and freely as she talked, as completely as she smiled, as wonderfully as she laughed.

He wished he had never seen her with Ivor. He wished he could stop thinking of her in that man's arms, in a position so similar to their experience on the wall walk.

Yet over and over he told himself it could only be lust he felt for the earthy Mair, and nothing more than righteous indignation that Ivor, as the captain of the guard, had not behaved with more circumspection.

Nor should Mair have shouted out in the courtyard as she had—what would people think?

Suddenly, the priest entered in a small cloud of incense. Trystan started and looked about guiltily.

At nearly the same time, his father limped into the spare stone chapel, escorting his mother. Trystan tried not to look surprised, but his father rarely came to mass. He had returned from the Crusade with little respect for supposedly holy men. Perhaps he had come to the chapel today because of their guests.

Trystan glanced at his father and encountered a look that told him his mother had revealed what he hoped.

So what was that expression he saw there? Dismay? Disappointment?

He would never understand his father. Had he not suffered and struggled his whole life so that his family would be successful? What could be more indicative of success than the marriage of his youngest son to the beautiful daughter of Sir Edward D'Heureux?

Trystan decided he wouldn't bother trying to comprehend his father's reaction. He would keep his gaze on the woman he hoped to marry.

How beautiful Lady Rosamunde was as she kneeled near the altar! The early morning light filtered through the windows fell on her pale, perfect face.

She looked like a statue. A beautiful, motionless statue devoid of vitality. A thing to be admired from afar, not passionately embraced with ardent desire.

And, he told himself, that was good.

The priest began to intone the Latin words and Trystan forced himself to concentrate on the mass. When it finally concluded, Trystan waited for his father and mother to leave before he moved, then he lingered near the door until Lady Rosamunde and her father drew near.

"How pleased I am to see you better this morning, Sir Edward." He bowed a greeting. "May I walk with you to the hall?"

"Certainly," Sir Edward replied as he started in that direction.

Trystan walked beside Lady Rosamunde. "May I speak with you alone after we break the fast, my lady?" he asked softly and, he thought, so that only she could hear.

"Anything you wish to say to my daughter you may say in my hearing," Sir Edward rumbled as he turned and glared at Trystan over his shoulder.

Trystan put a genial smile on his face as he quickened his pace to match that of the Norman. "Of course, Sir Edward. My father's solar will be free before the noon. Shall we meet there?"

"Very well."

As they continued toward the hall, Trystan spotted Dylan already in the courtyard, mounted on his prancing stallion and bidding the baron and his wife good-bye. Arthur sat on a smaller horse beside him, while nearby Dylan's guard prepared to depart.

A smile flitted across Trystan's face. If Arthur had not been sitting, he probably would have prancing with impatience, too.

"Farewell, cousin!" Dylan called when he saw Trystan and his companions. He bowed from his waist. "And a good day to you, my lord and my lady. Until we meet again."

"Farewell!" Trystan replied.

Dylan turned his mount and his party rode out the gate while his parents watched.

"Who is the boy?" Sir Edward asked.

"My cousin's son," Trystan answered.

"His *bastard* son," Lady Rosamunde amended, and Trystan heard the sneer in her voice.

As he glanced at her, he reminded himself that

he couldn't expect anyone raised in a Norman household to react in any other way.

"I see," Sir Edward remarked.

"He is the *younger* one. There are two," his daughter added.

"Unlike the Normans, we have never given so much heed to the legalities of a child's birth," Trystan explained calmly.

"But you must abide by Norman law now," Sir Edward said.

"We do, in our own way."

"Then is it indeed as I have heard, Sir Trystan?" Sir Edward demanded. "He will inherit, too, although he be a bastard?"

"As long as my cousin pays for that right, which we call *cynnwys*—inclusion. After it is paid, Arthur will inherit a portion of my cousin's estate. His elder brother will inherit the title. That is the way in Wales."

"Your cousin is a bastard, too, is he not?"

"Yes."

"Who paid for him to inherit?"

"My father."

"That's what I call a generous uncle, I must say," the Norman said in a tone that was both jovial and unnecessarily patronizing, considering that he had also shared the baron's largesse. "A pity for you though, isn't it?"

"Why should it be a pity if my father is gen-

erous and does what he believes to be right?"
Trystan inquired as they reached the door to the
hall.

"Why, otherwise your father would have more
to give his own sons."

Trystan paused as he reached for the latch, then
slowly turned to look at Sir Edward. "If that were
not the way in Wales, there is some doubt whether
my father would have anything to give his sons at
all. He is a bastard himself."

Sir Edward crimsoned. "I had forgotten."

As he caught Lady Rosamunde's embarrassed
expression, Trystan wished he had kept silent and
not let the Norman's condescending tone offend
him.

"Of course, my brother and sister and I are all
perfectly legitimate," he remarked evenly as he
held open the heavy door for them to pass.

As he did so, Lady Rosamunde's delicate,
flower-scented perfume encircled him, and she
gave him a little smile.

For once, it failed to move him. Nevertheless,
today he would ask her to be his wife.

"Are you nearly finished, Da?" Trystan asked
in what he hoped was a casual tone as he stood on
the threshold of the solar later that morning.

The solar was in the newest tower of his father's
castle. The room was smaller than some, larger

than others, yet very comfortable for all that. His
mother had seen to that, ensuring that it was
warmed by two braziers so that his father's leg
wouldn't ache with the chill. Cloth shutters on the
windows kept out cool breezes. Simple, yet thick,
tapestries lined the walls. The baron's chair sported
plush cushions, something he would never permit
on his chair in the hall, in case other men think he
needed coddling in his old age.

His father looked up from the parchment he was
perusing that lay spread open on his large table. "I
can be," he replied, beginning to roll the parchment up. "Do you want to talk to me about something? A young lady, perhaps?"

"Mother told you what I plan to do, then?"

His father's eyepatch rose with his quizzical
eyebrow, revealing more of the mottled scar beneath. "Plan to do? You still have not done it?"

"They are coming here soon."

"They?"

"Sir Edward and Lady Rosamunde."

His father grinned. "Planning to marry the old
man, too, are you?"

Trystan frowned. "Of course not, but he must
agree, so…"

"So you can kill two birds with one rock, eh?
Would you like me to stay, too, to tell them what
I think?"

Although his father's tone was not exactly serious, Trystan's brow furrowed nonetheless. "You won't object, will you?"

Now the grave expression of which his father was capable came to the older man's face. "If you truly want to marry this woman, no, I shall not object."

"Nevertheless, I would prefer you were not here."

"If that is what you wish."

"It is." Trystan felt relieved enough to smile. "I would prefer if *her* father were not here, either, but I have no choice."

"I could waylay him, if you like. I'm sure he could be persuaded to come with me if I offer to take him to Mair's brewery to sample more of her ale."

Did Mair, or her name, or her ale, have to intrude everywhere? "I would be most grateful."

"Very well. You wait here, and I shall do my best." His father rose and made his way to the door of the solar.

Then he hesitated and slowly turned around, a look on his face such as Trystan had never seen. "Your mother doesn't want me to say anything more, my son, yet I cannot keep silent."

He took a step closer, his one-eyed gaze studiously intense. "Do you truly love this woman? Do you honestly believe she loves you?"

Under his father's scrutiny, Trystan found himself swallowing hard. "I...I want to marry her, Father."

"That is not what I asked you."

"Can any man be sure if what he feels is love?"

"Oh, yes," his father replied with one brief, abrupt nod. "You'll know."

"Even if I am certain of my feelings, how can a man know what a woman feels in her heart?"

His father's smile grew rueful. "That is the great question, my son. What do you think this woman feels in her heart, about you or anything else?"

"How can I know? I am no seer."

"Has she said nothing of her feelings toward you?"

"She has made it her business to find out all she can about me, and our family."

"So would a merchant who thought to trade with us."

Trystan's hands balled into fists. "Did you ask Griffydd these questions? Or Dylan?"

"They were—"

"What? Different? Older? Better?"

"Trystan!" The baron strode closer and regarded his son soberly. "I do not think any man better than you."

"Really? Then why question my choice of bride? You did not interrogate them!"

"Griffydd was not at home when he fell in love,

and Dylan…'' The baron shrugged. ''Dylan is Dylan.''

''And I am Trystan, who wishes to marry Lady Rosamunde D'Heureux.''

His father's expression softened. ''Yes, you are Trystan, my beloved son, and I want nothing more than for my beloved son to be happy and content. That is why I ask these questions. Do you truly believe this woman will make you happy and content?''

''Yes!''

His father nodded. ''Then so be it. Ask her your question, and if she accepts you, your mother and I shall dance at your wedding.''

With that, he slowly limped from the room.

For the first time, it occurred to Trystan that his father was getting to be an old man. That was something easy to forget, for his father was as tall and straight as he had always been, his mind as keen, his eye as sharp, his laugh as boisterous. Indeed, even now, Trystan knew that if it came to a fight, his father would beat him not with strength and skill alone, but with a cunning years of fighting in the East had engendered.

Yet there was no denying that his father was no longer young, and so perhaps his attitudes were hardening with age.

Trystan took a deep breath and walked toward the window that overlooked the courtyard.

At least his father would make no trouble over his marriage, or his mother, if Lady Rosamunde accepted him. His brother and cousin would likewise have to accept his choice.

Suddenly, he saw his father come striding out the hall, Sir Edward in tow like a dog on a lead. A happy dog, Trystan thought, a smile coming to his lips. Or like a hound on the scent of game.

What would Sir Edward make of Mair? He had not spoken to Mair in the hall, or even looked her way once, Trystan didn't think. He had been so interested in the food and ale he had not watched the dancing, or he wouldn't have been able to miss Mair. She was an excellent, spirited dancer, and nobody enjoyed that activity the way she did.

A soft tap sounded and Trystan turned to behold Lady Rosamunde on the threshold of the solar. She looked about uncertainly.

"My father decided to go into the village with the baron," she said softly, a flush of embarrassment on her cheeks.

"Given what I have to ask you, I would rather be alone," he replied gravely. "Please, come inside and sit."

She glanced around the room as if still unsure.

"Leaving the door open, of course."

That seemed to reassure her and she glided gracefully inside.

"Please, my lady," he said, pulling a chair close to her.

Her gaze on the floor, she nodded and sat.

He had intended to begin with words of endearment and then, when he saw signs of encouragement, ask for her hand, but her attitude was rather disconcerting. She did not look at him even when he began to speak.

"My lady, although I am not worthy..." He cleared his throat. "My lady, I want you to know..."

Still she didn't look at him.

"My lady, do you like me?" he asked at last, his tone almost desperate.

He immediately cursed himself for a bumbling fool, until Lady Rosamunde raised her smiling face. "Your question is rather impertinent, Sir Trystan, is it not?"

"I would not ask it if it were not very important."

He held his breath as the rosy hue of a blush spread upon her cheeks.

"Yes, I like you very much," she whispered.

He went down on his knee before her and gazed into her beautiful face and tranquil blue eyes. Taking a deep breath and suddenly feeling as if he were stepping off a precipice, he said, "My lady, I beg the honor of your hand in marriage."

She smiled with pleasure—and a hint of what

might have been triumph deep in her eyes. "I would be honored to accept your hand, Sir Trystan, if my father gives his permission."

Trystan told himself the sick sensation he felt in the pit of his stomach was relief as he took her hands in his.

With sudden resolve, he swiftly rose, pulled her to her feet and gave her a hearty kiss.

"Sir Trystan!" she protested, pushing him away with more energy than she had ever demonstrated before. "What are you doing?"

"I am kissing my bride."

She adjusted her slightly askew cap and scarf. "We are not married yet!"

"No, not yet," he agreed. Then he smiled appealingly. "But surely I cannot be faulted for wanting to kiss my wife-to-be."

Her expression softened and he felt the tension begin to ebb from his shoulders. "No, I suppose not. You simply startled me."

He moved closer and spoke in a low whisper. "If I were to kiss you now, you would not be startled, would you?"

"No." She tilted her face up toward him, her eyes closed and her lips in an expectant pout.

She reminded him of a fish. A cold, dead fish. Nevertheless, he put his arms about her stiff body and kissed her again.

Her mouth was obviously and firmly shut tight,

and he did not even try to touch her lips with his tongue. He half believed she would squeal with horror if he did.

Once they were husband and wife, he assured himself, she would welcome his embrace.

"I shall speak to your father as soon as he returns. Do you think he will raise any objections?"

She moved away, walking toward the window. "He may." She turned around, facing him with an anxious look in her eyes and her hands clasped before her. "I will do everything I can to convince him of your worth."

"I would not have you in the middle," Trystan said truthfully. "I will convince him myself, if I must."

Lady Rosamunde sighed and her shoulders grew less tense. "I am sure you will, Trystan." She suddenly looked distressed. "You do not mind if I do not use your title?"

He shook his head, smiling gently. "No, I do not mind. Indeed, I am delighted to hear you say my name in any way at all. Will you ride with me this afternoon?"

"I shall be happy to," she said softly. Then she approached him and reached up to brush a kiss upon his cheek before leaving the solar. "My Trystan."

Standing in the storehouse of her brewery, Mair frowned as she sniffed her latest batch of short ale.

It didn't smell right, yet she couldn't figure out what was wrong.

She rubbed her forehead in dismay. Usually she could tell quite quickly if she had made an error, and exactly what was wrong, whether it was with the mash or the wort or the timing. Today, her mind was as cloudy as if she had finished off all the ale, not merely made it.

"Greetings, Mair!" a voice declared in Welsh from the open doorway.

She gasped and spun around, then relaxed when she saw that it was the one-eyed baron standing on the threshold, not his youngest son.

Smiling, she likewise replied in Welsh. "And greetings to you, Baron." Then she wagged her finger at him warningly. "But there will be no sampling today!"

"Not even a little?" he asked mournfully as he stepped inside the thick-walled, cool building. Sawdust covered the floor of packed earth, and rows of various barrels lined the walls. The scent of the fresh wood of new barrels joined with that of sawdust, ale and spicy mead.

"No, you may not taste even a little bit. Indeed, I would be ashamed to—"

She fell silent as Sir Edward D'Heureux appeared and entered after the baron. Out of breath, he panted heavily, although it was not so very far a walk from the castle.

"Oh, you have brought company," she noted.

"Indeed I have," the baron continued, still in Welsh, "for my gluttonous guest is quite fond of your ale." Then he winked. "I thought he might also enjoy some of your delicious *braggot*."

Mair frowned. "That's a heady brew for somebody not used to it."

"I think this fellow's had enough ale to be able to survive it."

"Who is this comely wench?" the Norman asked as he sauntered inside as if he were the king. He eyed her like livestock in the market, then walked around behind her. "She would be welcome to warm my bed."

Mair gave the baron a sour look. "He doesn't know I understand him, does he?" she muttered in Welsh.

The baron was trying not to smile. "No. Should we enlighten him, or let him prattle on?"

Suddenly Sir Edward grabbed her buttock.

Letting fly a Welsh curse, she spun around and glared at him before addressing the baron in Welsh. "I think you had better take this oaf back to the castle."

"God's teeth, she is a spirited female," Sir Edward noted, leering at her.

"Spirited enough to kick you and your illmannered derriere all the way back to the castle gate," she retorted in very passable French.

The man's eyes widened, then he frowned as he looked at the baron. "Do you allow your tenants to speak to a guest in such a way? How dare this impertinent creature address me in this fashion?"

"Impertinent, am I?" Mair said. "I am not the one grabbing somebody's *ffolen*. Not that any woman would want to grab your fat—"

"Alas, Sir Edward," the baron hastily interrupted, "I fear you have made a serious error. You've offended Mair, so likely there will be no more of that fine ale today, or any other day of your visit. It is never wise to insult the craftsman whose work you admire if you want more of it."

Sir Edward stared as if he had just been told she was really a woman. "God's blood, you cannot be in earnest!"

Seeing his dumbfounded surprise, Mair's annoyance fled. How could she be angry at such a fool?

With a companionable glance at the baron, Mair put her head in her hands. "Oh, woe is me! Sir Edward cannot believe it possible that I, a mere Welshwoman, can make such fine ale. Whatever shall I do? I must give up my trade and go weep by the river!"

With a wary and incredulous expression on his face, Sir Edward sidled cautiously toward the baron.

"This is a jest, is it not?" he whispered anxiously. "Or is she mad?"

Mair threw back her head and laughed. "No, Sir Edward, I am not mad. I am quite sane enough to make the best ale in Wales, if I do boast of it myself."

"She does," the baron confirmed, his tone grave but with a gleam in his eye as he surveyed the small barrels at the far end of the building. "Come now, Mair," he said, switching to Welsh, "we have had our fun, and he *is* my guest, so I think he must have some *braggot* in compensation."

While Sir Edward looked about as if he thought himself transported to a most bizarre kingdom, Mair said, "Very well, my lord. *Braggot* it shall be—but if he wakes complaining that he has a smith pounding on an anvil in his head, that his throat is as parched as the desert, and that he thinks he would be better off dead, I will not be held responsible."

"Thank you, Mair. I shall remember this."

"You will pay for this, too," she noted wryly.

"And so, I fear, may Sir Edward."

Chuckling, Mair proceeded to pour two cups of the *braggot.*

The baron made a great show of raising the drink to his nostrils and sipping before tasting; Sir Edward likewise raised his cup slowly, but his expression was more that of a man who fears poison.

Until he took a sip, and then he gulped the rest.

"God's teeth, this is marvelous!" he cried as set down the cup and looked at her expectantly.

"It is quite strong, you know," she remarked. "It is a mead mixed with ale, so—"

"This is fit for infants and children!" the Norman proclaimed. "Give me another!"

Mair smiled slowly as she filled the cup again. "Your order is, of course, mine to obey, Sir Edward. And you, my lord, will you have another?"

"I don't think—"

Sir Edward paused as he lifted his cup to his lips and let out a raucous laugh. "Too strong for you, Baron?" he asked mockingly.

The baron held out his cup as if he were accepting a challenge in the lists of a tournament. "Pour!"

Chapter Eight

"Oooohhh!"

The long warble of two decidedly drunken male voices, followed by snatches of inaudible lyrics, reached the ears of those assembled in the great hall of Craig Fawr well before the baron and Sir Edward stumbled over the threshold. They would have fallen, except that they had their arms around one another like old friends of at least thirty years standing. Or almost standing, at any rate.

The baron straightened, regarded those gathered in the hall, including Trystan and Lady Rosamunde as well as his own wife, and threw out his arm in a dramatic gesture.

"Shalu...sella...salutations," he slurred as he teetered precariously.

Then he grinned a lopsided grin and started to bow. He nearly fell flat on his face.

Trystan had never been more mortified in his life

as he hurried toward his father and Sir Edward, whose hair and garments were as disheveled as if he had been tossed in a blanket.

Nor had he ever seen his father so drunk before. He had heard stories, of course, of a time or two when his father had over-imbibed in his younger days, but he had never been a witness to such an event. Indeed, his father generally held men who did not know when to stop drinking in contempt.

Until today, apparently.

As Trystan reached his tipsy parent, he glanced over his shoulder at Lady Rosamunde, whose face was as red as her gown while she sat motionless in her chair. He knew his face must be just as red with shame.

"Da, you're drunk," he muttered as he put his shoulder under his father's for support.

"My son, I am," he confessed happily.

"No, you're not," Sir Edward slurred, patting the baron on the back. "You're just...well-greased!"

The plump Norman burst into a low rumble of a laugh at his own wit.

"Emryss, you are going to retire at once," Lady Roanna said with a firmness of tone that all obeyed, even the baron, as she hurried forward.

Her husband waggled his eyebrows in a comical leer. "With you?"

"Emryss!"

"Da, you're making a spectacle of yourself!" Trystan chided as he tried to disengage his father from Sir Edward's bear-like grip.

Another swift glance at the still sedentary—and no doubt horrified—Lady Rosamunde only increased his disgusted dismay.

Sir Edward tried to point an accusing finger at Trystan. Unfortunately, it seemed he couldn't quite focus.

"Young man," the Norman said, leaning forward as if hinged at the waist, "tha's no way to shpeak to your father, the very best of men. The very best of companions." Sir Edward sniffled and his eyes filled with tears. "The very best friend a man could ever have!"

"Trystan, help your father to our chamber," his mother ordered, although the lift at the corners of her lips belied her stern tone. She signaled for one of the soldiers to come forward. "We shall help Sir Edward to his."

"Nonshense!" the Norman roared. "It's the shank of the evening!"

One of the maidservants went by bearing a tray of mugs of ale. Sir Edward grabbed one, took a swig, smiled—and then promptly bent over and lost it, and more besides.

Trystan looked again at the dais and realized that Lady Rosamunde was gone. He didn't blame her for being too embarrassed to stay.

Here he had been hoping to tell his father his good news, and instead his father had gotten Sir Edward drunk and humiliated them all. If Lady Rosamunde decided she wanted nothing more to do with him, or his family, he would not be surprised.

If he felt any relief, it was that Sir Edward appeared to be even more drunk than his father.

"Come, Da, to bed," he ordered, not aware how much like his mother he sounded at that moment.

If his father noticed, he gave no sign.

"Away, ho, to bed we go!" the baron caroled as Trystan helped him stumble toward the tower stairs, leaving his mother and the soldiers to look after Sir Edward.

It took some time to get his father to the bedchamber, a time made longer by his father's insistence on pausing at nearly every stair as he attempted to remember the lyrics of the *pwnco* he had composed the morning after his marriage to Lady Roanna. It was a wedding poem, each verse made up on the spot, and in response to a similar impromptu verse from those gathered outside the bridal bedchamber.

"And then Gwillym said something about the length of my sword," his father mumbled meditatively, scratching beneath his eye-patch with one finger. "My sword or my staff or my root or something..."

"Oh, Da," Trystan muttered. He had heard this too many times to be remotely interested. Right now, all he wanted to do was get his father to his bed.

"Those were the times, my son!" the baron cried as he started forward again. "Not much of a wedding night because I was an idiot, but I made up for it later!"

"Yes, Da. Watch that worn place."

"And I'll never forget the look on your mother's face when I threw that door open and her standing there nearly naked—"

"Careful!"

"Whoo! I'll get that loose bit fixed tomorrow. Good times we've had, my son. Great times. There's nothing like a good wife. Nothing! Now that Lady Rosamunde, she's fine if you like 'em cool and skinny."

Trystan's jaw clenched. They were nearly there.

"No fire banked there. Not like your mam!" The baron leaned on the frame of the bedchamber door and regarded his grim son as he swayed. "But Sir Edward and I are such great friends now, he won't object."

"I am glad to think some good might come from this disgraceful behavior, provided Sir Edward remembers you were such a great drinking companion tomorrow."

The baron looked shocked. "Remember? Why,

of course he will! And I'll wager he'll remember not to accost Mair like that again, either,'' he finished before he careered into the room.

Trystan followed. "He accosted Mair?"

"Well, he tried." The baron started to chuckle as he drew off his patch, revealing the empty eye socket and mottled scar beneath. "God's wounds, you should have seen his face when he found out she made the ale... You should have seen hers when he grabbed her!"

"He touched her?"

His father tried to undo his belt. "Aye, he did." He paused, his expression soddenly pensive. "Not that a man could blame him. She's got a very nice *ffolen.*''

"Da!"

"Well, she does." The baron finally got his belt off and sighed, and scratched. "I'm half-blind and love my wife, but I know a shapely bottom when I see one." He eyed his son. "You sound upset."

"Who wouldn't be upset to see his father come staggering home like the village drunkard, having set the man he hopes will be his father-in-law drunk, too?"

"I am not to blame if the fellow doesn't know his limits. We tried to warn him about the *braggot,* but he wouldn't listen. Since he's a guest, what could we do?"

"You could have said, 'No more.'''

"I could've." The baron began to struggle with his tunic. "Where's your mam?"

"Seeing to Sir Edward, remember?"

"Oh, aye." He gave up with his tunic and sat heavily on the bed, then fell back. Trystan headed for the door. Let his mother deal with his father.

The baron sighed heavily. "Poor Mair."

Trystan slowly turned back. "What do you mean, poor Mair? Was she upset by what Sir Edward did?"

"Not after a minute," the baron replied thickly. "You know Mair. Flares up and dies down as quick as a blink."

Trystan took a step toward the bed. "Then why 'poor Mair'?"

His father yawned.

"Because she's got nobody."

"She has Arthur."

"Who will be going to Fitzroy for his training next year."

"Fitzroy?"

"Aye, of course, like Dylan and you and your brother. Who else?"

"I thought Dylan—"

"Dylan wouldn't be tough enough with his own son, and Genevieve would fuss over him and spoil him. Trefor goes next month to Fitzroy, and Arthur next year."

Trystan hadn't thought of that. "I've heard she has Ivor."

"*Had* Ivor, and he had her, but not any more."

Trystan tried not to look as if this interested him in the least—and told himself it didn't. "How do you know?"

His father yawned again and as he spoke, his words drifted off. "I'm the lord, that's how. A lord has to know these things..."

Then he snored.

Trystan was very tempted to wake him, but he didn't. After all, it didn't matter to him if Mair and Ivor were no longer together. Indeed, if he was glad, it was only because there would be no more shameful couplings in the courtyard. Or on the wall walk, either.

Fighting the arousal that always and apparently inevitably came with that recollection, he quickly and quietly left the room. As he shut the door, he heard his mother's footsteps approaching and forced his thoughts to bathing in freezing water as he waited.

Unfortunately, that made him remember Mair in the river.

He thought of the time Fitzroy had kept him standing out in the cold rain because he had left a spot of rust on his armor.

That worked better, and by the time his mother reached him, he was more calm and composed.

"He's asleep," he announced quietly.

"No doubt he'll sleep late in the morning and be sick when he wakes."

"You're not angry?"

His mother gave him one of her rare smiles. "In all the time I've known him, I think I've seen him drunk five times. I can excuse this lapse, and I think you should, too."

"Because it is so rare that he disgraces us so?"

Her brow wrinkled. "No, because I'm sure he got drunk keeping Sir Edward company. Don't you want your father and Sir Edward to be friends?"

"He might have found a better way."

"I cannot argue with that, but he will be punished enough tomorrow."

Trystan smirked, remembering the one and only time he had imbibed too much *braggot*.

Once had been more than enough to teach him the foolishness of that.

"You're right. I'll never forget—" He caught himself. "I remember the night Dylan got drunk and nearly fell off the roof of Mair's brewery."

Nor would he forget how Mair had roundly chastised him for letting Dylan climb up in that condition. Then how she had started, stared and burst out laughing when she realized he was just as staggeringly, stinkingly drunk.

It had been months before she had stopped teasing him about it, or ceased to ask him how he had enjoyed sleeping in the empty water trough where she had left him.

"Mother?" he said as she put her hand on the door latch.

She turned back to him, a quizzical expression on her face. "Yes, my son?"

"Do you think Sir Edward will be upset about this tomorrow?"

"No. I daresay your father could not have selected a better method of ensuring his agreement to your marriage if he had called a council."

Trystan wondered why he wasn't more pleased by this observation. Perhaps he was too tired after the strain of this day and this evening. "Good night."

His mother reached out and gently caressed his cheek. "Good night, my son. I suppose you'll sleep well, for it seems you will get the bride you desire, after all."

"I daresay I will."

Lady Roanna sighed softly as she watched Trystan trudge down the stairs. He set such high standards for himself, and everybody else, her youngest boy. If only he could have a little more of Dylan's natural *joie de vivre*, his life might be easier.

But then he would not be Trystan.

As she quietly entered the bedchamber, her husband sat up. "Angry as a hornet, my son is," he noted calmly, and without a trace of drunkenness.

His wife frowned and put her hands on her slender hips. "I thought you were drunk."

Emryss grinned. "So did Trystan."

"What manner of joke is this? He's very upset with you."

Emryss rose and drew off his tunic, exposing his naked torso covered with several battle scars. "A man may be excused for saying many things when he's drunk that would be intolerable if he were sober."

"Emryss!"

"Well, it's true, is it not, love of my heart?"

"What, then, did you say to him?"

"Not a lot. Just a little reminder or two."

His wife's eyes narrowed. "About what?"

The baron strode over to the basin and splashed cold water over his face. "Who."

"About who, then?"

He dried off his face before answering somewhat sheepishly. "Mair."

"Mair!"

"Who else? Angharad says—"

"I know what Angharad says, and I also know that Trystan wants to marry Lady Rosamunde. You should not interfere."

"But he doesn't love her!"

Roanna sighed and pulled off her cap and scarf,

then shook out her long hair that was yet more dark than gray. "That doesn't mean he loves Mair."

"She loves him. She's loved him since she was a girl."

Sitting by the small table where she kept her brushes and mirror, Roanna started to brush her hair. "She told you that, did she? Today, when you and Sir Edward were drinking? I find that difficult to believe."

"God's wounds, of course she's never told me. She's never told Trystan, either, or he wouldn't be mooning over that Norman baggage."

Roanna stopped brushing and twisted around on her stool. "You really don't like Rosamunde, do you?"

"Not a bit, and especially not after an afternoon with Mair."

"She is not noble," Roanna reminded gently, very aware that her husband had always liked the boisterous, joyful Mair, who never seemed to let her troubles get the better of her.

"As if I give a fig for that! She is perfect for Trystan, she loves him and I think if Trystan would quit thinking about outdoing Griffydd and Dylan, he'd realize that, too."

"It is difficult being the younger son. And if he decides not to marry Lady Rosamunde, that doesn't mean he'll wed Mair. He may think…"

She cleared her throat delicately. "He may think he would be taking Dylan's leavings."

"Surely to God he's smarter than that."

"We are speaking of matters of the heart, my love, not the head."

"And it is of his heart I speak! He could scarce keep his eyes from Mair the other night when she was dancing, even though that pale Norman creature was by his side. He looks daggers at Dylan like a jealous lover. By God, Roanna, I've been waiting for him to come to me all defiant and proud and tell me he was determined to wed Mair although she was not noble, and I could go to hell if I thought I could stop him." He stopped and stared. "Roanna, are you crying?"

"I am," she admitted sheepishly, wiping her eyes and trying to smile. "I...I wish he would marry her, too, Emryss. I do not like Lady Rosamunde a bit, no matter how hard I try, and I fear she will make his life miserable. Mair would make him happy—although they'd probably quarrel like cats and dogs—but we *mustn't* interfere. Trystan is a grown man, and although it breaks my heart, he must marry as he sees fit."

The baron went to his wife and pulled her into his comforting embrace. "I know, my love, I know. But perhaps I have given him something to think about. If not, I will have to live with the rumors that the baron is losing his ability to know when he's had enough *braggot* in his old age.''

Mair sighed. It was long past time to retire, and yet she couldn't seem to summon the energy to get up from the stool before the fire. Instead, she stared into the glowing embers, thinking and remembering.

She had lived in this little house all her life. Here her mother had borne her, and then died. Here her father had raised her, teaching her all that he knew about brewing before he, too, died, when she was a girl of thirteen.

Here she had been when the DeLanyea boys had come with their father to talk to her father about ale for the castle.

Grim Griffydd, so much older and wiser.

Merry Dylan, who always made her laugh.

And Trystan, with those soulful eyes and that wonderful smile, a smile that made her feel she had won a great contest if she could provoke it.

How she had longed for him to come, even though he scarcely said a word on those visits! She had teased him and teased him to try to get him to speak.

Perhaps she would have done better to let him stay silent. Then he might have liked her more.

If Trystan had liked her, she might not have tried so hard to make the other lads in the village like her. She might not have been so delighted to discover that they did, and she might not have given in to the other delights they provided.

If she had not been so hurt by Trystan's animosity, she might not have been so happy when Dylan responded to her advances. Of course, then she would not have Arthur, and she would be all alone.

Just as she was alone now while Arthur was with his father. Just as she would be alone when he went off to become a knight. After that, he would never live here anymore. He would be but a visitor.

A tear rolled off the end of her nose and she sniffled.

"Mair?"

"What?" she demanded, jumping up and whirling around to see Trystan at the entrance of her house.

The light of the full moon seemed to illuminate him like a halo, as if he were an angel in mortal form.

A ridiculous notion. She knew full well he was merely a man, albeit a handsome, passionate one.

A handsome, passionate one she should be angry with, she reminded herself. "What do you want—and at this hour of the night?" she demanded sternly.

"I...I couldn't sleep and had to speak with you."

It wasn't fair that he was looking at her like that, as if he needed her as much as it was possible for one person to need another, not when he had his *other plans.*

"Something that was so important it couldn't wait until morning?" she asked. "Or do you want to emulate that Norman and get drunk, too? Mind, it'll be difficult, for a child could hold his drink better than that fat, impertinent lout."

Trystan came inside her house and closed the door behind him, enclosing them in an intimacy that was both dreadful and exciting, as if she were caged with a dangerous beast that would not kill her, but could nevertheless wound her greatly.

As he already had.

"My father told me that Sir Edward…touched you."

"Touched? That is a mild way to describe it. He grabbed hold of me as if I were a hunk of meat hanging on a rack." She eyed him skeptically, and he could not blame her for that reaction to his unexpected visit. "So, are you here to apologize? That's more than he had the manners to do."

"No, that isn't why I've come." Trystan took a deep breath, then looked down at his belt buckle as he fiddled with it, unable to meet her steadfast, brown-eyed gaze.

Nevertheless, he must and would continue. "I came to tell you that Lady Rosamunde has accepted my offer of marriage. All we need now is her father's approval, and I do not think he will withhold it.''

''How kind of you to tell me,'' she remarked disdainfully.

''I didn't want you to hear it from anybody else,'' he admitted. ''I thought…I thought I owed you that much.''

Something flickered in her eyes, like a spark being doused. ''Thank you.''

At her soft words, he took a tentative step closer. ''I hope you can understand what her acceptance means to me, Mair.''

''I fear I must be slow-witted, sir, because I would have assumed it meant you are delighted. There is, then, some other reason you are pleased? Vanity, perhaps?''

As he came closer, he ignored her harsh remarks. It was more important that he say what he had to say. For reasons he could not voice, he wanted her to understand.

''I crave something that even my father, for all his influence and power, cannot provide,'' he confessed. ''I want more than to be famous here in the borderlands of Wales and England, as my father and brother and cousin are. I want to be accepted in the court, in London. To be noticed by the king. To do that, I *must* have a Norman wife, a noble wife.''

If he thought he saw any other emotion but disdain flash in her eyes, he decided he was mistaken when she spoke. "How convenient, then, that Lady Rosamunde is both. I am happy for your success."

"But do I have your understanding, Mair?" he persisted. "Can you see why I must succeed? Can you understand that it is not easy having the relations as I do, to be at the end of such a famous line?"

"At least you have a line to be the end of," she muttered. "But I suppose it is not easy being a DeLanyea."

He didn't pay so much attention to the words, for he was overjoyed by the hint of sympathy in her voice.

She understood why he had to marry Lady Rosamunde.

"I've been thinking about something else," he continued quietly, still gazing at her intently as he came closer. "Mair, I was wrong to tell you that I would not acknowledge a child if it appeared to be mine. That would be dishonorable, and cowardly, and I do not wish to be either. So, if in some months time—"

"Oh, Trystan!" she sighed raggedly as she turned away.

"If in some month's time, you have a baby and it resembles me…"

He fell awkwardly silent when he realized her

shoulders were shaking, as if she were silently sobbing. He went to her and took her by the shoulders, gently turning her to face him.

She wiped her damp face brusquely with her sleeve.

"Mair, I'm sorry," he whispered as he held her lightly by the shoulders and gazed down at her sorrowfully bent head. "I didn't mean to upset you. I thought you would be relieved to hear that I intend to do the proper thing."

She raised her tear-moist face. "Oh, Trystan," she repeated, this time with more of her usual determination. "Are you blind or stupid or both?"

Puzzled, he made no response.

"Has it not occurred to you that you need not fear that?" she asked, roughly pulling away from him. "Have you never noticed that I have not borne another child after Arthur, although I do not live a celibate life?" That gleam of defiant pride that made her Mair returned to her eyes, with even more brilliant vitality. "Trystan, obviously I cannot have any more children, or I would have by now."

Her words hit him like a strong wind and he actually staggered. "Oh, God, Mair, I didn't think—"

"Do you ever?" she demanded. "Do you ever think beyond what you want, what you think you need?"

"Of course!"

"If it pleases you to believe that."

"I admit I didn't think about your lack of children until tonight—but surely you cannot fault me for that!"

"Does it never occur to you that just because a person doesn't parade their pain, they have none?"

"Mair, I'm sorry, but I am not a seer."

"Thank the Lord. One in the village is enough."

"I don't want to talk about Angharad."

"Neither do I." Her defiance suddenly seemed to melt away like snow in sunlight. "Trystan, I do not fault you for not thinking about whether or not I can have more children. Nor do I fault you for going after what you want, if you think it will make you happy. Forgive me. I am...tired."

He stared at her, horrified to note her pale face and the shadows beneath her eyes. "You are not ill?"

She laughed softly, and never had he been more pleased to hear that musical sound. "No, I am not ill. Just tired, I assure you." She made an insolent little curtsy. "Although I note your concern and thank you for it. It was difficult work keeping your future father-in-law supplied with *braggot*. He drank nearly all I had."

He smiled in relief, and more. "My father kept pace with him well, I gather."

She looked surprised, her glowing, lively eyes

widening. "He only had two cups the whole time he was here."

"And that was enough to set him drunk? Good God, perhaps *he* is ill."

"He was perfectly sober when he left here. Indeed, he had to be, because he all but carried Sir Edward back to the castle."

"But he was singing—or trying to—and he staggered into the hall like the worst of sots... I don't think it's very funny, Mair."

At the sight of his stern and annoyed expression, she tried to stifle her laughter. "I wish I had seen your face!"

Trystan's expression remained grim. "I fail to see anything funny about my father pretending to be adle-pated with drink. Nor can I understand why he would do such a ludicrous thing."

"Oh, take the sword out of your backside, Trystan! It's obvious he wanted to spare Sir Edward the shame of being unable to hold his *braggot*. No one will say a word about *him* if they think the baron was drunk, too."

Trystan blinked. "Oh."

"Oh," she repeated teasingly, her eyes dancing in the dim light and her mouth forming an enticing circular pout. "Not so disgraceful, your father, is he now?"

Trystan started to smile.

"And mind, your father is paying the bill, for

which Sir Edward should be very grateful. I never saw a man drink like him. No finesse at all.''

''No finesse and no manners, either, and I do apologize for his behavior.''

''Well, your father and I had a good laugh about it, so no harm done. Mind, if he touches me again, I'll hit him.''

Trystan's face grew serious. ''Mair, that would not be just. You hit too hard.''

''Oh, I do?'' she demanded. ''Then how be I just tap him like this?''

She stepped toward Trystan and raised her hand as if to strike him lightly. Before she could, he caught her wrist and stared into her questioning brown eyes.

Chapter Nine

"Oh, Mair," Trystan said wistfully, "why do you make me feel this way?"

Very aware of the slight pressure of his long, strong fingers, she swallowed hard.

"What way?" she whispered, her gaze searching his face.

"As if I must kiss you, or die."

"I...I do not want you to die," she stammered softly. "I suppose you had better kiss me."

His eyes widened and then, with a low moan of surrender, he did.

How he kissed her! As a drowning man seeks to breathe. As a sick man yearns for a cure. As a blind man wishes to see, or a deaf one to hear his beloved say his name.

He was not alone in his burning need, for Mair knew she might never again have a chance to be with him. He was going to marry that Norman woman, and soon after his father would give him an estate, and so he would be gone.

Gone to another woman's bed, to her arms.

Gone as if dead.

Her mouth claiming his, she held him tight, memorizing the taste of his lips, the scent of his skin, the feel of his strong embrace. She reveled in the way they seemed made for each other, for so their bodies matched, breasts to chest and hips to hips.

And more.

Her whole body throbbed with desire, a desire that burned as bright as lightning illumines the night sky.

How she wanted him! If not forever, for this last time.

His caresses grew more fevered as he felt her relax into his arms. Oh, how he wanted her! She was fire and light and spirit, giving all and holding nothing back. She was all that a passionate woman should be, and more.

Yet soon he must wed another. Soon, but not now. Now he had Mair in his arms, to hold and kiss and love.

His lips left hers to trail hot kisses down her chin and neck as she arched back. Her hands gripped him tight as he nuzzled her bodice lower so that her breasts were exposed to his lips and his tongue.

How perfect she was! Like a goddess. Not a

cold, untouchable goddess, but a warm, living one, the embodiment of all a woman could and should be.

"Make love with me, Trystan," she panted. "Please. Just once more. Love me."

He knew he should not. He had asked another to be his wife. He himself had made the decision.

But he was only a mortal man, and he could not refuse her request, not when every particle of his heart and body urged him to love her.

He lifted her in his arms and carried her to the bed, laying her upon it.

"Trystan." She sighed.

Then he was with her, his body covering hers, his weight on his knees between her parted legs, and on his hands as he looked down on her. Her thick hair spread upon the pillow like a living corona, and her face was flushed with longing.

And in her eyes...in her eyes was all any man could ever hope to see in a lover's eyes.

"Love me, Trystan," she repeated, running her hands up his arms to stroke his shoulders and chest. "Love me so that I will never forget. Love me so that when I am alone and lonely, I will have the memory of you to warm me again."

"I will never forget you, Mair. No matter what happens or where I go, I will keep a special place in my heart for you."

Telling herself it was enough, she pulled him down for a passionate kiss.

The touch of his lips on hers again ignited her. And him.

With the same passionate abandon of the other times, they loved. Hands tore at clothing, caressed, held, stroked. Naked flesh met naked flesh and the sounds of their sighs and moans filled the darkness.

After a time, Trystan joined with her and they began to move as if one body, never to be separated. Until, in one exquisite moment, they both cried out with release.

Sighing, Trystan lowered himself and laid his head on Mair's sweat-slicked breasts. His breathing slowed and it almost seemed as if he would sleep there, content.

While Mair turned her head away so that he wouldn't see her tears.

At that moment, across the village, Angharad suddenly sat bolt upright in her bed, her eyes wide as she stared at the vision that came from she knew not where.

And then she smiled.

The first faint streaks of dawn were turning the sky orange and fuchsia when Trystan awoke. Mair slumbered beside him, her naked body soft and warm against his, one arm thrown over her eyes, her thick, curling, wondrous hair brushing his naked arm.

He lay back and stared at the ceiling.

What had he done? How could he have been so stupid, and so blind?

How could he have been so ignorant of the desire in his own heart?

To believe he loved Rosamunde…to convince himself he didn't even like Mair…

But there could be no going back. He had asked and received Lady Rosamunde's hand. To try to break that promise now would be dishonorable of him and humiliating for her. She had done nothing wrong, and Mair believed this was the last time they would be together.

Sighing, he rose cautiously so as not to wake Mair. Let her enjoy the innocence of sleep.

As he looked down at her in the rosy light of dawn creeping in through the small window, he realized how beautiful she was, from the top of her chestnut-haired head to the soles of her slender feet. He had always thought her pretty, but never had he noticed the perfection of her features. The smooth texture of her skin. The shape of her eyes. The straight bridge of her nose, with those delightful freckles scattered across it.

He turned away and dressed quickly. He had lingered here much too long as it was.

He had to think of the best route back to Craig

Fawr, a route where no one would see him sneaking back like a thief.

He would go by the river, then around the village past Angharad's house, and so that way. If questioned, he would say…would say…

He would pray he would not be asked.

Ready to leave, he hesitated and gave himself the pleasure of one last look at the still-sleeping Mair. He very much wanted to kiss her good-bye, but he dare not.

For if he did, he would surely want to stay, and that he could not do.

Lady Rosamunde leaned yet closer to her father's ear. She spoke softly, although there was no one nearby. She had dismissed the maidservants, yet she didn't trust them not to linger and listen outside the door. All servants were untrustworthy gossips. "You drunken sot! You ale-guzzling, despicable reprobate! I know you're awake, so stop trying to pretend you're not. I hope you die!"

Her father groaned and covered his eyes with the back of his hand. His hair lay dank and limp, and his stale breath nearly made her gag. "My head hurts as if fifty demons are poking it with spears."

"More than your head would hurt if I had my way," his daughter softly snarled.

"I am ill."

"No more than any other drunken man would be the morning after." She grabbed his hand and thrust it away so that the sun shone full on his red-rimmed, squinting eyes. "How could you do this to me?"

He twisted his head to avoid the light. "You are not the one with the aching head."

"No. I am the one who must marry or else we will have to fall on the charity of the church. And what help do I get? None!"

"Rosamunde, it was that woman. She kept pouring," he whined.

"What woman?"

"The alewife, the one they called Mer. Or Martin. Or something like that."

"Mair," she corrected impatiently, remembering well the woman who had borne a son to the young baron.

"Yes, her. An impertinent wench."

"She did not welcome your advances, I suppose." Her accusation was but a guess; however, when he didn't answer right away, she knew she had surmised correctly.

Over the years, her mother had paid out enough money to sobbing women, as well as enraged fathers and husbands, to prevent a charge of rape for Rosamunde to have no delusions about her father's honor in that realm.

She leaned toward him again. "You stupid, stupid oaf! What did the baron make of your attempt at seduction?''

''No harm was done.'' Her father opened his bleary blue eyes and regarded her as if he were an innocent victim. ''We are friends. I went with him for your sake, Rosamunde, to try to discover how he felt about the marriage.''

She made a skeptical frown. ''And you had to get drunk to ask? Well, what did he say? Does he favor it?''

''I...um, yes!''

''Liar. You never asked him.''

''Rosamunde!''

''I know when you are lying, Father, so please do not bother to try it again.'' Sighing, she sat on the bed and stared at the stone wall opposite. ''I hope you are right. I hope you have done no harm.''

''I think—''

She rose abruptly. ''I don't care a whit what *you* think. It is what the baron thinks, and the baron's wife, and his son that I care about. Now I am going to go see if I need mend any breaches.''

''Send in a servant, will you? I need—''

She didn't hear him finish, for she closed the door firmly. Glancing about to make sure no maid was watching, she locked the door.

When she went below, she saw that she was

right to be so cautious, for one of the snooping maidservants was at the bottom of the steps.

"My father will sleep for the rest of the day and should not be disturbed. I will check on him later and send for you if he requires assistance."

The maidservant looked as if she understood, although Rosamunde suspected she didn't speak French very well. Nevertheless, as long as she understood Sir Edward was to be left alone, that was enough.

Rosamunde smiled to herself as she proceeded to the chapel. Let her father be a little hungry and very thirsty for the rest of the day, and then maybe he would learn to watch the amount he drank.

Her smile grew when she saw Trystan striding toward her across the courtyard.

How wonderful he looked this morning, tall and strong and young! Although he was dressed in a plain dark tunic and breeches, he looked as fine as any noble of the court. Even better, he lacked the arrogance that spoiled most men who could compare for looks or status.

She swiftly studied his face, wondering what he thought of her father's behavior.

He looked...different. Stern. Unyielding.

That was not a good sign.

When he reached her, she did not have to try very hard to look upset. "I am so sorry for my father's state last evening," she began softly.

"And I am equally sorry for *my* father's actions," he replied as he bowed. "Perhaps we could talk about last night after the mass?"

"If you wish."

"I think we should."

As Rosamunde placed her hand on his arm, she felt her trepitation grow until it was as if her stomach were filled with rocks. Where had her devoted suitor gone?

Had her father's drunken behavior altered things so much? If it had, she would add this to the list of all the things for which she held him accountable, and he would pay. By God, how she would make him pay!

She scarcely listened to the mass as the priest proceeded. The greater part of her attention was focused on Trystan, standing so straight beside her. He looked more like his father now than she had ever noticed before, yet without that exuberance that seemed so much a part of the baron. Trystan seemed grim, and older somehow, as if something had aged him in the space of a night.

Suddenly, she felt frightened. What if he no longer wanted her? What would she do? She had to marry. She had waited long enough as it was for a man who had money and power, a man who wouldn't pry too closely into her family's finances, a man who didn't make her flesh crawl at the thought of his intimate caress.

Now she had found him and won him. If Trystan wanted to break their betrothal—yes, their betrothal. He had asked for her hand in marriage, and she had accepted. An honorable man would be bound by that promise and, she realized with a sigh of relief, the DeLanyeas were said to hold their honor very dear.

Nevertheless, it could be that Trystan was having second thoughts. Therefore, her father must agree to the basic terms of the marriage agreement as soon as possible. Today.

When the mass was finally over, she allowed Trystan to escort her to the hall.

"My father is not his best this morning," she began when they sat, "but I think he will soon recover. I did not see your father at mass."

Trystan shook his head. "He was not there, or my mother, who stayed in their bedchamber to nurse him. He rarely drinks overmuch."

Rosamunde demurely lowered her head as she struggled to think of what to reply. She could hardly say the same of her father, for any man who had witnessed how he had enjoyed the ale of Craig Fawr would know otherwise.

"I'm sorry my father didn't take better care," Trystan said softly, and tenderly. "I am sure he would have if he had known how upset you would be."

Now she knew how to proceed, and her heartbeat quickened as she picked up the napkin and dabbed at the corners of her dry eyes. Naturally a man like Trystan DeLanyea would want to be his lady's protector. He would want to see himself as saving her from her ogre of a father.

In that, he would not be so far wrong.

But it was not the time to think of her father. It was time to protect her own interests.

"He can be a beast," she whispered with a pathetic catch in her voice. "Oh, Trystan, I fear I am too upset to be with all these people. May we not go somewhere else? Somewhere private?"

Trystan nodded and rose, holding out his hand. As he led her to the solar, she surreptitiously looked about at the other few guests who still remained at Craig Fawr. She didn't know them well, for they were mostly Welshmen with Norman blood, or Normans with Welsh blood like the DeLanyeas. There was little chance their gossip would spread very far, and certainly not to London.

Trystan escorted her to one of the sturdy chairs and waited while she sat. Then he said, "My lady, truly, there is no need for you to be so troubled by your father's behavior. It is I who should be troubled, for my father never should have taken Sir Edward to the alewife's."

She rose and put a long, white finger against his sensual lips. The unexpected sensation of his warm breath and firm mouth both startled and thrilled her. "I do not blame the baron. He did not know my father could not be trusted to act properly in such a place. I deeply regret that I did not stop him from going."

Trystan moved away and flushed, and she was pleased that her touch affected him so. "He suggested the visit for my sake."

"Your sake?" she asked, a furrow appearing between her delicately arched brows.

"I wanted to be alone with you."

A look of sudden understanding came to her smooth and flawless face. "To ask for my hand?"

"Yes." His gaze seemed to intensify. "If you wish to make a different answer now, I shall understand."

She put her face in her hands and started to weep. Years ago she had learned that tears could be an effective weapon on either parent, and she was glad to have that skill today.

"You do not want me anymore!" she wailed piteously. "Oh, what shall I do? Who will help me now?"

Trystan hurriedly knelt at her feet. "My lady!"

"I was so happy to think I was finally going to be safe! That you loved me and would take me away from that brute. That I could be free of the fear."

"Why do you fear your father?"

Her shoulders still shaking and her face still hidden by her hands, she said, "He beats me when he is drunk."

In truth, he was as helpless as a babe when he was drunk, but Trystan didn't know that.

Trystan slowly rose and when he spoke, she could scarcely believe it was the same man talking, so hard and cold did his voice sound. "Did he strike you last night?"

"Yes," she said softly as she wiped her face with the edge of her sleeve. "I have bruises on my arms."

That was a lie, of course, but surely he would not demand to see the marks.

Trystan looked down at her lowered head and heard the catch of breath as she tried to stop crying.

He had asked this woman to be his wife, and she had accepted. Honor demanded that he abide by that acceptance, no matter how much he wished it could be otherwise. Knowing how her father treated her, he certainly could not abandon her.

"You will be safe from him from this day forward, my lady. I will never allow him, or any man, to lay a hand upon you. And you will be my wife."

It was a promise and a vow, and if it also felt like a death sentence, he had only himself to blame for being so filled with ambition and the need for an advantageous marriage, he had ignored his heart.

"Oh, Trystan!" she cried, standing and throwing her arms about him in a way that seemed almost passionate. "Thank you!"

He could not bring himself to return her embrace.

"Your chivalrous response makes me love you more. Indeed, I think my father should be well enough this afternoon for you to speak to him of our marriage." She tilted her head and smiled at him, a smile that no longer moved him. "I am going to be very bold and demand a kiss from my husband-to-be."

He obediently complied.

"I shall see how my father is. I cannot abide any long delay before the marriage agreement is made. Farewell for now, Trystan," she said with another pleased smile as she left him. "I will tell you when you may speak with my father."

"Farewell," he replied as she swept from the room.

Then he sat on the table, his shoulders slumped, and ran his hand through his hair.

He was caught in a trap of his own making. He had asked, and Rosamunde had answered in good faith. To break that betrothal, even though he had yet to seek her father's permission, would be an act of dishonor.

It was not Rosamunde's fault that he had not listened better to his heart. Last night, looking down into Mair's familiar face, noticing the vitality he always felt in her presence before it gave way to the overwhelming passion she roused within him, he knew that he belonged with her, and she with him.

Before, all he had heeded was his ambition to make a finer marriage than his brother and cousin.

Yet what of children? He had always longed to be a father. Mair could not have more children.

When he chained himself to Rosamunde, he would have to take comfort from the hope that she could.

And if it proved otherwise, perhaps it was a just punishment for his foolish determination to be more famous than his brothers and father.

That afternoon, Baron DeLanyea tried to look pleasantly surprised as Sir Edward, Lady Rosamunde and Trystan approached while he sat in the hall resting his aching leg and scratching Mott's head.

Sir Edward looked as sick as a man who had imbibed too much *braggot* ought to look. Although her cheeks seemed slightly flushed, his daughter had that blank, lifeless expression she always did.

But Trystan's visage, which was decidedly grim, brought a genuine smile to his face. Perhaps Sir Edward had refused to give the young couple permission to wed. If that were the case, the baron reflected happily, he might get truly drunk in celebration.

Then Sir Edward's lips turned upward in what was obviously supposed to be a look of genial bonhomie, and Baron DeLanyea felt his heart sink.

"Good afternoon, Sir Edward, Lady Rosamunde," he said in as friendly a tone as he could muster.

"A good afternoon it is, if you concur with my agreement to let your son marry my daughter, and we can come to terms," the Norman replied amiably.

The baron wondered what the devil was going on. After all that Trystan had said before, he should look as if he had just been awarded the crown of Wales. Instead, he looked like a man condemned as a traitor.

He realized Sir Edward was regarding him expectantly.

"Ah, indeed!" he declared, forcing himself to sound delighted. "I cannot say I am surprised. What young nobleman would not want to marry your beautiful and graceful daughter? Shall we go to my solar and discuss this happy news?"

"Very well," Sir Edward agreed.

The baron looked at his son. "Will you join us?"

"Yes."

The baron then smiled at Lady Rosamunde, who

reminded him rather uncomfortably of a cat who had just swallowed a mouse. "I am sure Lady Rosamunde has no wish to be bothered with the monetary aspects of matrimony. I shall have Gwen fetch my wife, and you two can discuss the details of the wedding feast, wherever it shall be."

"Oh, I would be so pleased to be married here, in Trystan's home," Lady Rosamunde quickly replied. "I fear our chapel at home would be much too small."

The baron had negotiated with too many traders not to comprehend what her response really indicated.

She, or her father, or both of them together, didn't want to incur the expense of a wedding feast.

God's wounds, what he wouldn't give to turn back time and never invite Sir Edward and his daughter to Craig Fawr!

"We shall be delighted to have the wedding here," the baron finally answered with a courteous bow. "My wife especially will be pleased."

At least that was true enough, the baron reflected. "And I'm sure she will be eager to hear all you have to say on the subject, my dear," he said. "Now, if you will excuse us, we men should get to the business of marriage."

If the baron was any judge of character, and he was—rather unfortunately, he thought, in this particular instance—she was not happy to be consigned to the petty details of the ceremony and the feast.

He frankly didn't care. He wanted to try to discover what his confusing son was thinking, and the only way he was going to get even an inkling of that would be to get him away from his future bride.

"Gwen," he called out to the maidservant who had entered with an armload of fresh rushes for the floor, "take Lady Rosamunde to my wife, who I believe is in the cellar checking on the quantity of flour. Then bring three goblets and a carafe of wine to my solar."

As he led the others to his private room, the baron hoped his youngest son would provide some explanation for his less-than-delighted demeanor when he had apparently achieved his cherished desire.

Somehow, though, he didn't think that likely.

Chapter Ten

The next morning, Lady Rosamunde smiled as she strolled through the rose garden of Craig Fawr. Only a few blooms remained, and the frost had touched those that did. The dry branches scratched the stone walls, and the ground was hard beneath them.

Over the wall, the sun shone dimly through the gray clouds that seemed to promise rain at any moment. The air was chill, yet not so very cool in the sheltered garden. A few birds warbled their songs, the sound high and bright above the usual noises of a busy castle.

In truth, however, Lady Rosamunde paid little heed to her surroundings, for she was congratulating herself on the success of her plan.

Yesterday, the baron had agreed to pay nearly four hundred pieces of gold for her bride price, as was the Welsh custom.

Even better, a large portion of that money would come directly to her, not her father, for so he had agreed when she had told him of her plan. Her dowry was a small amount of land outside London, and household goods that had been her mother's. Those had cost her father nothing. As for the land, it was not much, and that nearly useless, as the bridegroom would discover soon enough. Naturally she would feign ignorance and cast the blame onto her father who she hoped she need never see again after she was married.

Why should she? she mused with a scowl clouding her lovely face as she pulled her fur-lined cloak more tightly about herself. What had he ever done for her, save these negotiations?

As he described the discussion to her later, he had been obviously surprised by the ease of the negotiations, until she suggested—to his even greater surprise—that for the baron, his son's happiness was of the utmost importance, not making the best bargain.

Her smile disappeared when she recalled how dumbfounded he had been at that notion.

He, and his notions, didn't matter anymore, she reminded herself, because the agreement had been written and signed. She had won her prize.

"My lady?"

Startled by the deep and unfamiliar male voice, she whirled around to see the captain of the guard standing near the entrance to the garden, his helmet and gauntlet gloves held loose in his large, powerful hands that could probably snap her in two like a twig. His long, barbarous hair ruffled in the slight breeze, and his furrowed brows added to his savage look.

Her heartbeat quickened as he approached, his chain mail jingling ever so slightly from his athletic stride.

She raised her chin haughtily, a thrill of pleasure running through her when she saw that the muscular fellow was wary of her. "Who are you and what do you want?"

"Ivor I am, my lady, and captain of the guard of Craig Fawr," he said, his Welsh accent much stronger than Trystan's. His voice was deeper and rougher than Trystan's, too, and strangely rather pleasing.

She realized he was impertinently, if secretively, studying her body and a new, exciting, unfamiliar warmth spread through her.

"Well, Ivor, what do you want?" she asked, her tone slightly more genial.

"I thought you should know something about Trystan."

"*Sir* Trystan."

He nodded. "Sir Trystan, then. The man you're going to marry."

"Yes, I am, and I have no interest in gossip."

"I have told no one else what I saw."

Her stomach did a strange little flip at his grave assertion.

"Come," she said, leading him as far from the entrance as possible, so that no one could see or hear them.

No one could see or hear them. It was an exhilarating realization.

She turned to face the soldier, noting the breadth of his shoulders and the strong, clean line of his jaw. "So tell me, Captain of the Guard of Craig Fawr, what did you see?"

"Sir Trystan leaving a woman's house in the village."

She raised an eyebrow.

"In the small hours of the morning. At dawn."

"When was this?"

"Yesterday."

The day Trystan was so grim and unlike himself.

She turned away, trying to think what this might mean. Trystan had apparently spent the night in the village. He was a young and vital young man, and she had given him no outlet for his passion. No doubt he had spent the night with a whore, seeking release.

He was but a man, after all.

"Forgive me for upsetting you, my lady," Ivor said close behind her, "but thinking you ought to know, me."

She slowly faced him, looking up at his anxious eyes. His lips. ''I thank you for your concern, Ivor. Please do not tell anyone else what you saw.''

''As you wish, my lady.''

He made no move to leave, and neither did she. Then suddenly he took her hand and pressed a kiss upon the back of it.

His firm hold and gentle kiss excited her more than anything Trystan had ever done, and her limbs seemed to soften like warm butter.

''I...I think you had better go, Ivor,'' she whispered, pulling her hand away, albeit reluctantly.

''Forgive me, Lady,'' he said as, with a look of dismay in his dark eyes, he backed away.

Then he turned and fled from the garden like a man pursued by hounds thirsting for his blood.

While Rosamunde remained behind, panting as if she had run up every step of one of the watch towers.

As she tasted the sip of ale, Mair glanced out the door of her brewery, noting the height of the sun in the sky. The day was fine and sunny, unlike the past several that had been cold and wet, the rain like heaven's own tears. Traveling would be easy and even pleasant on a day like today, and for that, she was glad and grateful.

The long fortnight of Arthur's absence was over, and he would return with Dylan today.

She had never known a longer fourteen days, and she couldn't deny that the official announcement of Trystan's betrothal to Lady Rosamunde had not made them pass any quicker.

Since she had heard the news, she had busied herself with her own business and avoided going to the castle unless it was absolutely necessary. She didn't want to see Trystan, or the lady.

This ale was excellent, she concluded, good enough for a knight's wedding feast. Good enough to be included in the order the baron had made for that very event, another month from now.

Maybe she should add an emetic.

Anwyl, she was getting peevish in her old age, she thought with a self-deprecating grin. She had wanted Trystan to love her one last time, and so he had. She had said she wanted nothing more but the memory of being in his arms, and she would have to abide by that. She could not go begging for his love now, or ever.

The light from the door dimmed. Angharad stood on the threshold in all her haughty, raven-haired glory—Angharad of the striking features and regal bearing, who had had no man after giving the young baron a son.

Angharad, who supposedly had the Sight.

And who, for a shock, actually looked to be smiling pleasantly.

"Good morning, Mair," she said, sauntering in

with that queenly grace that Mair had been jealous of forever.

"Good morning, Angharad. What brings you here today?"

"Arthur is returning today, is he not?"

"Aye, with Dylan."

Angharad sat uninvited on an empty barrel. "Dylan is going to take Trefor back to Beaufort with him for a last visit before Trefor goes to Fitzroy for his training."

"I know," Mair said, wondering what had really brought Angharad here.

"So, Trystan is marrying Lady Rosamunde."

"Aye, you were wrong about that, I see."

"No, *I* see," Angharad said with the superiority of manner Mair had always hated.

Even bearing Dylan a son herself had not made her equal in Angharad's eyes.

But what, after all, did Angharad have to brag of, except bearing Dylan's first child? She was still an unmarried woman who spun wool for her keep, of the same rank as Mair.

"What do you 'see'?" Mair demanded, not troubling to hide her skepticism.

Angharad made an inscrutable little smile as she adjusted her woolen shawl. It was a thing of dark blue beauty, for there was no denying that Angharad's wool was of the best quality. "Something that will please you."

"Oh, and I should trust to this latest vision? It will be more likely to occur than my alleged marriage to the baron's youngest son?"

"Trystan isn't married to that Norman yet, you know."

"The agreement has been made, written and signed. Unless she changes her mind, or dies, he would never break it."

"She is a woman, and so like to change her mind."

"Why is it you are so good at telling everybody else their future, and never speak of your own?"

Angharad's eyes flashed. "You know why. I cannot see it."

"How convenient."

"That is the truth. I have never had a vision about myself."

"*Anwyl*, Angharad, I am not going to marry Trystan, so if that's all you care to talk about, I have things to do."

Angharad made no move to rise. Instead, her cryptic smile widened. "You are going to have more to do next summer."

"It doesn't take the Sight to guess that, if business is good."

"It has nothing to do with business. How are you feeling these days, Mair? Tired? Tender in the breasts? A little sick to your stomach?"

"I feel fine. No more tired than usual, no more

tender about the breasts than I normally am at this phase of the moon, and my stomach doesn't trouble me a bit,'' she declared truthfully, fighting the surge of wild hope Angharad's questions had engendered.

"Well, then you may have an easy time of it this time."

"An easy time of what? Brewing?"

Angharad laughed softly. "One could call it that."

"Oh, you and your riddles! Have you nothing else to do today but come by and annoy me?"

"I thought you would be happy to know for certain."

"To know *what* for certain?"

"That you are with child."

"Angharad, don't!" Mair snapped as she flushed hotly. "Don't be cruel."

"I thought you would be happy with what I've seen."

Mair drew in a deep, ragged breath. "If it were true, I might be."

Angharad stood and regarded Mair steadily, a truly warm smile on her face. "Mair, it is true. You are with child, and Trystan is the father. He will be a strong, healthy son, Mair, and when he is grown, he will be a credit to his parents."

Mair sat heavily. "That's…that's not true. It cannot be true."

But oh, her heart sang unbidden, what if it were? What if her desire to hold a baby in her arms again was going to be fulfilled?

If she were pregnant, of course it was Trystan's child. She had not been with Ivor since her last woman's time.

But how would Lady Rosamunde feel about that? She would not be happy, and would likely make Trystan's life a misery.

She might even break the betrothal, and all Trystan's fine plans would be ruined. He would be humiliated.

He was so proud, he would find that nearly unbearable.

And because of that pride, he would likely hate her for destroying his ambitious hopes.

"If I am with child, it could be another man's," she suggested.

"No, it is not," Angharad affirmed. "I have seen it."

"What, Trystan and me? You are mad."

"No more than you. I tell you, I have seen you with him."

"Oh, you have taken to sneaking about the village spying in windows, have you?"

"You know what I mean."

Yes, Mair knew. And she knew that if Angharad told people of her vision, everyone in and around Craig Fawr would believe it was true.

They had all believed Angharad when she had predicted that Mair would marry Trystan, despite their apparent animosity. Indeed, they had been so certain of it, and that the truth would upset her, that they had kept it a secret from her for a long time.

"Don't tell anyone, Angharad," Mair asked, as close to begging as she had ever been in her life. "Please. He is to be married to that Norman, not me, and no good can come of telling him."

"You will not be able to keep it a secret, Mair."

"The name of the father I can, and I will."

"Ivor will think—"

"Ivor will know it cannot be his."

"Ah!" Angharad said, nodding. Then her brow furrowed. "Yet who will you say—"

"I will not say. I will smile and laugh and tell them to guess. If you keep silent, no one will suspect Trystan, of all men. Will they?"

Angharad shook her head. "But he should know he has a son. Would you deny him that knowledge? And your son should have his birthright as a knight's firstborn."

"I would spare his bride the knowledge. Have you seen her? Can you imagine the life she would lead him if she knew?"

"She is not going to marry Trystan."

"Oh, Angharad, stop!" Mair cried, her hands

balling into white-knuckled fists. "I don't believe your prophecies! I am not such a gullible fool!"

Angharad's pale face crimsoned. "Then how can I be right so often?"

"You make good guesses, that's all. Look you, Trystan is betrothed to that Norman, and he's going to marry her. I don't know how you knew about Trystan and me. Maybe you saw him leave, or somebody else did. Or maybe you think you know, but you're not as sure as you pretend to be."

Angharad's gaze faltered.

"Oh, God!" Mair moaned softly as she scrutinized Angharad's downcast face. "That's the truth, isn't it? You really don't know the future for certain." Her voice trembled. "Maybe...maybe I'm not to be blessed with another child, after all."

Angharad rose and grasped Mair's hands, her gaze frank and sincere. "Mair, I do believe what I see. But I don't reveal everything because sometimes I cannot be absolutely sure what my dreams mean.

"I will admit that I'm not certain who Trystan will marry. One day he said something nasty about Dylan, so I named the woman I thought would most upset him. I had my revenge when I saw how that enraged him, but I shouldn't have been so flippant.

"I confess I did not consider how you might feel about it."

"Angharad, I, of all people, know how Trystan can make you want to say something to get his goat."

"Mair, I do know Trystan will marry, and he will be happy with his wife. And I know he will have sons, and a daughter. I know that the child you bear is his," she finished firmly.

"After so long, Angharad, to have a baby," Mair said wistfully before resolve appeared in her eyes. "Please, say nothing to anyone. Let me deal with this, in my own way."

"But you should not deny your child his birthright."

"I would not make trouble between Trystan and his Norman bride if I can help it."

"Since you bear his child, you already have," Angharad pointed out as she walked to the door. She paused on the threshold and looked back. "I shall do as you ask, Mair, because our sons are brothers, and I've always liked you. Indeed, I am truly happy for you, because you have wanted another baby for so long."

Mair nodded as Angharad departed, then sat down on the empty barrel to stare unseeing as she thought of all that had been said.

Another baby at last! Trystan's baby. She would have a part of him to love and cherish forever.

He had said he would acknowledge their child— but would he really? When it came to choosing

between peace with his Norman wife or acknowledging his illegitimate child, what would he decide? Should she even force him to make that
choice, or should she do it for him?

And what of Arthur? He had been her only child
for so many years. He might resent the baby even
more than he resented Ivor.

She would have to ensure that didn't happen,
and she would have to ensure that her second son
did not feel as Trystan did, bitter and resentful and
always second-best.

That might not be easy, especially if she kept
the identity of his father a secret from him. But to
tell anyone…

The whole village might find out, and then rumors would go from village to village, and eventually Lady Rosamunde would hear.

It could be that by that time, though, Trystan
and his wife would have a child of their own.

Under Norman law, her child would be a bastard
and entitled to nothing unless Trystan paid the
cynnwys. Yet the child she bore to Trystan should
have rights of inheritance, as well as the issue of
his marriage with Lady Rosamunde. To keep the
identity of her child's father a secret would be to
rob him of his birthright.

Eventually, she would have to decide if she
should spare Trystan and rob her own child of what

was rightfully his, or tell the truth and let Trystan deal with the consequences.

Perhaps there could be some arrangement made, a secret arrangement, so that Trystan could provide for his son without officially acknowledging him. It was not an honorable way, but it was better than nothing.

"Mam!"

Smiling, Mair rose and held out her welcoming arms as her son ran through the door, tossing his leather pouch onto the floor nearby. Behind him, at a more sedate pace, came Dylan.

She hugged Arthur tightly to her. "Oh, I've missed you! Were you a good boy?"

"I learned how to knock Da down!" Arthur exclaimed proudly as he disengaged himself from her maternal hold.

"Aye, and too well, too. I am bruised from head to toe," Dylan said ruefully, shaking his head with apparent regret.

"You don't look bruised," Mair noted.

"I *feel* bruised."

"You didn't answer my question, Arthur," she said as she retrieved his pouch, knowing that Genevieve would have sent him home with all his linen clean. "Were you a good boy? Did you mind your manners?"

"He was as good as I expect my son to be," Dylan replied.

Mair laughed. "*Anwyl,* that could mean nearly anything!"

"I was good, and chewed with my mouth shut and remembered to use my napkin and I said please and thank you and I only took third helpings six times."

Mair cocked her head studiously. "Ah, only six?"

"Come now, Mair, Genevieve practically force-fed the lad. He did very well."

She smiled warmly and ruffled her son's dark hair. "I am glad to hear it. Now take your things to the house, Arthur."

Her boy hurried to obey. As he left the brewery, Mair sighed happily, glad to have him home again.

"You're looking well," Dylan remarked.

"Not too tired?"

He gave her a quizzical look. "Should you look tired?"

"No."

"You look very happy."

"I am—to have my son home again. I miss him when he's gone."

Dylan continued to scrutinize her in a way she found disturbing. "What are you staring at?" she demanded. "Is my dress torn? My hair more of a mess than usual? Did a tooth fall out without me knowing it?"

"You're...glowing."

"Oh, so now I am an oil lamp? Maybe I've been eating too much fish."

"It's a nice glow."

"I've been tasting the ale, perhaps a trifle too much."

Dylan chuckled. "You had best take care, Mair, or you'll wind up drinking all your money away."

"Not me," she declared.

"Good," he replied with a grin. "Now, if you will excuse me, I had better go see Angharad and Trefor, or Trefor will be accusing me of playing favorites." With a wry expression, he shook his head. "I fear I am doomed to that accusation for the rest of my life."

"It seems to be a common enough thing among brothers."

"How would you know? You never had any."

"As I seem to recall you saying, I got eyes. I've seen enough brothers to have an opinion."

"Well, I shall bow to your wisdom." He sauntered toward the door, his easy stride reminding her of Trystan. "Arthur said he wants to come, too, if that's all right with you." His voice dropped to a conspiratorial whisper. "I suspect he wants to try knocking Trefor down."

Then he grinned. "And good for him, too. The boy needs taking down a peg or two, even if he is my eldest son."

"I won't disagree."

"Will I see you in the hall tonight?"

"No, not tonight. I want to have Arthur all to myself after he's been away."

Dylan grinned and nodded, then left her alone.

Later that night, after the ladies and most of the household had retired for the night, Dylan and Trystan lingered by the glowing embers of the hearth, a mug of Mair's fine ale in their hands.

"Well, and best wishes, is it?" Dylan said.

"I thought you were intending to ignore my betrothal."

"No, not at all. I gave my best wishes to the lady earlier, when you were with your father giving Ivor the watchword for tonight."

"You did?"

"Aye," Dylan replied lightly. "She seems a modest creature, I must say."

Trystan frowned. "I hope you weren't rude."

"Me?" Dylan asked innocently. Then he continued truthfully. "Not at all. I said I hoped you would both be happy. She smiled and nodded. That was it."

"Good."

"Easily upset, is she?"

"She is a proper lady," Trystan replied stiffly.

"Ah, well, and a beauty, no doubt of it. How much was the *amobr?*"

"This is no place to discuss such things."

Dylan glanced at the few men on the other side of the hall bedding down for the evening. "*Anwyl*, boy, I'm sure she'll be worth it."

Trystan gave him a sour look. "Must you be so crude? And stop calling me 'boy'!"

"God's wounds, Trys! Still as prickly as a bear with a thorn in his paw, you. I thought you'd be dancing on air with happiness since you've got your prize."

"I am happy. I just don't see the need for discussing the bride price or the dowry with—here!"

"With me, you mean?" Dylan said.

"Very well. With you."

Dylan shrugged. "If you think so." He took a gulp of the ale, then wiped his lips with the back of his hand. "Then tell me this. Who is Mair sleeping with these days?"

"God's wounds, Dylan, I'm not some ancient crone to be gossiping about people," Trystan growled, staring down at the frothy beverage.

"Oh, come you! I just asked a simple question."

"Why don't you ask Mair?"

"I will. And then I'll ask her when her baby's due."

Chapter Eleven

"Baby?" Trystan demanded in a harsh whisper, not willing to believe this could be true, or if it was, that Mair would not have told him.

"Aye. At least I think she's with child. She's got that glow to her face. I asked her about it, but she didn't—" Dylan paused and a puzzled expression came to his handsome face. "She's just having a baby. It's not as if she's done murder."

"Did she tell you she was with child?"

"No." Dylan got a warning look in his eyes. "You're not going to be nasty about this, are you? I know you don't approve of the way she chooses to live. *Anwyl*, I should have kept my mouth shut."

"*Anwyl*, yes, you should," Trystan said, getting to his feet and glaring at his cousin. "If Mair was with child, she'd tell you, wouldn't she? You two are thick as thieves. You always have been. If she's not, how can you talk like this when you're not sure. You're worse than a gossiping old crone, you are!''

"No need to get so—"

"You'd better keep your mouth shut about babies or suspicions of babies unless she tells you she's with child for certain. Good night!''

With that, Trystan set down his mug with a bang, then marched off toward his chamber.

Dylan watched him go as he leaned back in his chair. A wry smile twisted his sensuous lips.

"Well, well, well,'' he muttered softly.

Then he raised his mug in a salute in the direction of Angharad's house. "Well, Angharad, I am going to have to beg your pardon. All this time I thought you were having your own little jest at Trystan's expense. Now I find it is not so impossible, after all.''

"Mair!'' a voice whispered in Mair's ear as she slept.

She awakened in an instant. Opening her eyes, she sat up and peered in the deep darkness at the man standing beside her bed.

"Trystan?'' she whispered. "What in God's name—?''

"Hush! Arthur sleeps above, does he not?''

"Aye, he does. What do you want?''

As she waited for his answer, she realized he wore no cloak, only his usual dark tunic and breeches, a heavy belt about his narrow waist. What made her heartbeat quicken, though, was his look of impassioned determination. ''I need to talk to you. Come with me. Please.''

''In the middle of the—?''

''Yes!''

He sounded so desperate, she made no protest as she climbed from the bed and wrapped her blanket over her thin shift. ''We can go to the brewery.''

She went to the glowing embers of the hearth and lit one of her candles in a brass holder. Candles were expensive and she reserved them for rare and special occasions.

She sensed this was just such a time. And she wanted to see his face more clearly.

Clutching her blanket with one hand and holding the candle aloft with the other, she regarded him studiously.

He looked as serious as death.

''Here, take this while I get my shoes,'' she ordered in a hushed voice as she handed him the candle.

Their hands touched for the briefest of moments, and she struggled to ignore the sensations even that aroused while she sought her shoes and slipped them on. The stiffness of the leather against her feet seemed to remind her that this was no dream, but an unexpected reality.

"Now we can go," she said.

He nodded and led the way, and she closed the door softly behind her.

Outside, the night was chilly, and the moon and stars obscured by scudding clouds. The branches of the trees in the wood nearby bent and moaned with the wind. Ahead, Trystan cupped the fluttering, feeble flame with his hand.

She had to nearly run to keep up with him, yet dared not ask him to slow down. She didn't want to make more noise than necessary at this hour of the night.

After they entered the brewery, he set the candle on the top of a pile of small casks, then, motionless, watched her enter and close the door behind her.

The brewery smelled of ale and honey and the spices she used for *braggot* and mead, a homey smell that usually comforted her. Tonight, it only seemed to remind her of who she was, and the higher status of the man facing her.

Despite the difference in their rank and all that had passed between them, Trystan was still the most attractive, compelling, honorable man in the world to her, a man whose embrace she craved with an almost physical hunger.

Yet now his brow was wrinkled with concern, his mouth a grim line, his eyes in shadow. "Dylan says you are with child."

She bit back a curse. It was too soon even for her to be absolutely certain, despite Angharad's firm belief. Angharad must have broken her word to keep quiet, and that realization added to her anger and dismay. "Why does he think that?"

"He claims he can tell by your 'glow.'"

"Nothing else?"

"Nothing else," he confirmed.

"Then why would you believe him?"

"Because he knows women well. And others also claim to be able to do the same. My father's old nurse said she could tell the day after a child was conceived by the look in a woman's eyes, and she was never wrong."

"You would credit Dylan with that same skill, then."

"Aye, I would."

"I don't."

Trystan's expression grew anxious in a way she had never seen before. "If you were with child, and the child mine, you would tell me, wouldn't you?" he asked softly.

She could not lie to him, not with him looking at her that way. "It's early days yet to be sure."

Trystan lowered his head as if deep in thought. Or shame.

"Would you want to know, Trystan?"

He raised his head. "What?"

"Would you want to know? I do not have to say, especially if doing so would cause trouble."

His eyes grew as hard as flint. "If I am the father of a child, I want to know."

"Under any circumstances?" she pressed, determined to be certain.

"Under *any* circumstances," he grimly affirmed.

"I have not been with Ivor since my last woman's time, so if I am with child, he is yours."

"He?"

"Angharad says I am to have a son."

"A son!" His expression softened. "Our son."

Oh, how her heart soared to see that look! "Yes, our son, Trystan," she agreed softly. "I will have another baby after hoping for so long."

His visage hardened, reminding her that he came from a race of warriors. It was a look to strike fear in the heart of an enemy, and to make her suddenly afraid. "I am betrothed to another. The contract has been written and signed."

Confused by this change in him, she responded with hasty assurance. "You need not claim him outright, Trystan. I will understand if you would rather not. As long as you make some provision for him, in secret if need be, I will be content."

Trystan's harsh visage lightened a little. "If you bear me a son, I will claim him."

"Truly?"

Sir Trystan DeLanyea drew himself up proudly. "I will claim him, and he shall have what rights and privileges he deserves as my son."

She had to ask. "Under Welsh rules, or Norman?"

His gaze faltered, and he became again the boy she had known. The boy she had fallen in love with, and still loved.

"An inheritance and title don't matter so much, Trystan."

"They do to me—and they do to the Normans."

She straightened her shoulders and spoke frankly, as one warrior to another. "I say it *must* be so."

She went to him and took his hands in hers. "Trystan," she said firmly, "you know Lady Rosamunde better than I, but do you honestly believe she will not begrudge a child of ours anything, even to the air he will breathe? Do you not see that she will do all in her considerable power—and that of her family—to destroy him? *Anwyl*, Trystan, you wanted to be wed into a powerful family, and so you will be. Now you must reap what you have sown."

His grip tightened as he regarded her just as steadily. "And do you honestly believe that I would let anyone—*anyone*—cause harm to a child of mine?"

He let her hands drop as he stepped further back

into the shadows. "If it comes clear that you bear my child, come to me and tell me. I will acknowledge him—or her—as an honest man should. As a Welshman should."

She sighed, knowing he would keep his word. "Thank you, Trystan. What of Lady Rosamunde?"

"I will deal with her," he said grimly.

"How?"

"Let me worry about that." He started for the door. "Good night, Mair."

"I do wish you joy in your marriage, Trystan," she managed to say evenly.

He turned again to look at her. "Mair, Dylan told me what you said, about why you didn't marry him. Is there no man you have loved enough to marry?"

What would he have her answer, this man who already belonged to another? Who was betrothed to the woman he had chosen, the daughter of a rich and powerful man who had the means to elevate Trystan to the highest rank in the land?

A rank Trystan deserved, for he was the best of men.

She was nothing but an alewife.

Yet oh, how tempting it was to tell him how much she loved him! That she had always loved him, and would never love another. That she had only gone with Dylan and those others because she thought Trystan would never care for her.

It was too late to tell him that.

She shook her head. "No, Trystan. I have not yet found a man I could love enough to marry."

"I see."

He left her as silently as if he were a spirit.

After he was gone, she took the candle and made her way back to her house. She could hear Arthur snoring softly as she blew out the candle and returned to her cold and lonely bed.

Standing beside the road leading to Dylan DeLanyea's castle where they had come to bid their father farewell, Trefor turned to his half brother.

"I'm going to Fitzroy before you," he noted loftily.

"Of course you are," Arthur said with a trace of rancor. "You're older. I'll come in the spring."

"I suppose you're extra glad of that now."

"Of course. I am to be a knight."

"No, that's not what I meant," Trefor replied with his usual cryptic superiority.

Arthur snorted with disgust and turned to leave him.

"Don't you want to know what I mean?" Trefor demanded.

In reality bursting with curiosity, Arthur halted. "Then say what you mean, you *gnaf!*" he charged.

"I meeeean," Trefor said, drawing out the word as an additional torment, "with all the noise a baby makes, you'll be glad to be away."

"What baby?"

"Don't you know?"

Arthur's hands balled into fists. "Know what?"

"Your mam's having a baby."

"She is not."

"She is too!"

"Is not!"

"Is too!" Trefor asserted.

"My mam isn't having a baby. She would have told me if she was!"

"Are you calling my mam and our da liars?" Trefor demanded, his arms akimbo. He was taller than Arthur by a head, and had the broad DeLanyea shoulders and lean, muscular build.

But then, so did Arthur.

"I heard them talking myself," Trefor continued.

"Listening at doors like a sneak."

Trefor flushed. "I wasn't!"

"You were, too! You've always been a sneak!"

"I'm not!"

"Are too!"

"Am not!"

"You are—and I'm going to tell my mam you're spreading lies about her!"

"It's true! My mam *knows!*"

That gave Arthur a moment's pause, a pause Trefor was quick to exploit. "Our da knows, too. He can tell by their faces, he says. You know he wouldn't lie."

Even as dismay and dread filled Arthur's smaller frame, he squared his shoulders defiantly. "So who's the father, then, if your mam's so wise?"

It couldn't be that Ivor; he hadn't come round for days and days.

Trefor's lips curled up into a nasty smile. "Wouldn't you like to know?"

That was all Arthur could take.

Too angry to speak or even think clearly, he flew at Trefor, knocking the bigger boy down. He sat on his chest, pummeling his half brother as Trefor struggled to shove him off.

"Arthur, stop!" Trefor cried. He tried to cover his face with his arms as the surprisingly strong blows continued to rain down on his head. "Arthur, I yield! I *yield!*"

Panting heavily, the words finally registered and Arthur lowered his hands.

"It's Trystan."

"Who?" Arthur mumbled through the haze of his exhausted fury.

"Trystan is the father," Trefor repeated. "At least that's who my mam says."

"And our da?"

"He said he didn't believe it at first, but he does now."

Slowly Arthur climbed off his half brother.

It had to be true. If his father and Trefor's mother said it was so, it had to be.

And he himself had seen Trystan leave their house after being alone with his mother. He had heard his mother crying in the night. Those things had puzzled him at the time; they didn't anymore.

"You're not going to tell your mam I told, are you?" Trefor asked anxiously.

Arthur slowly shook his head as he walked away.

"Where are you going?"

Arthur didn't answer.

Nor did he, or Trefor, see the horseman who had slipped from his mount to hide behind the underbrush, and listen.

Trystan stared down at the chessboard and tried to concentrate on the game. In truth, he was but an indifferent player, preferring outdoor sport to chess and other such amusements. His father, Dylan, Sir Edward and others had gone hunting, but Lady Rosamunde had not been in a mood to ride today.

Thinking of possible confrontations to come, he

had decided to remain behind with her. She had suggested chess, and he had complied.

They were not by any means alone in the hall. Maidservants came and went, bringing refreshments to the tenants who had business with his father and were awaiting his return. Giggling and whispering like giddy birds, they also cleaned the hearth and laid a new fire, replaced burned-out torches in the sconces on the wall, laid new rushes and sprinkled herbs.

They were really rather distracting, but even if they had been utterly silent and as inconspicuous as the wooden furnishings, Trystan knew he would still be losing the chess game.

Lady Rosamunde was a remarkable chess player, despite her efforts to make it look as if she were not. She could blush and demur all she liked, yet there was no mistaking the competitive gleam in her eye.

His father had been wrong to say Lady Rosamunde had no spark. She had a spark, all right, when she wanted to win, and Trystan surmised that was every game and every time she played.

Even now, he could tell that she had planned her move well before she made it, hesitating only to add to the impression that she wasn't sure what she was doing.

He, on the other hand, took his time because he could barely concentrate on the game.

Most of the time he was thinking of Mair, and her child.

Her possible child.

His possible child.

Their possible child.

Over and over again, he recalled their conversation last night.

She said she had loved no man enough to marry. Not Dylan, not Ivor, and apparently not him, either.

Surely it was better he know the truth. After all, what would he have done if she had said she loved him? As she had said, he had allied himself with a powerful Norman family; to break an agreement with them would have disastrous consequences, and not just for him. Dylan had rightly pointed out that what Trystan did could affect the rest of his family, too. Although his father also had powerful and influential friends, Trystan was not sure their help could outweigh the damage Sir Edward could inflict.

No, he had set his course when he had asked Lady Rosamunde to be his wife.

"How is it that the king moves again?" she asked, looking at him questioningly with her large, limpid blue eyes.

Patiently, he told her, while inwardly he wondered how he could ever have thought her more lovely than Mair. Mair's eyes were stars of light and laughter; Rosamunde's eyes seemed greedy and shrewd.

If Mair did have his baby, he hoped he would have Mair's lively brown eyes. And freckles, like fairy kisses across his nose.

He realized Rosamunde was looking at something behind him. Judging from the curl of her rosy lip, she wasn't pleased to see it.

Wondering what in his father's hall could bring that expression to her face, he twisted to look over his shoulder.

With a very determined look, Arthur marched toward them, oblivious to the curious regard of the maidservants and waiting tenants.

Trystan couldn't fault them for staring. It was rather obvious Arthur had been in a fight. His hair was disheveled and muddy, his cheek bruised and both knees of his breeches were torn.

"I have noticed your people tend to lack a certain respectful attitude," Lady Rosamunde observed quietly, "but how can this urchin have the gall to come into your father's hall in this bold manner?"

"Arthur has every right to come here," Trystan explained. "He is my second cousin and Dylan's second son."

"Oh, yes, one of your cousin's wild oats in the flesh."

Trystan didn't reply; he was more interested in

what had brought Arthur there, and with such a look on his young face.

Glowering at Trystan and ignoring Rosamunde, Arthur came to a military halt beside the table.

"Yes, Arthur?" Trystan inquired.

"I want to know if it's true," the boy demanded in Welsh.

Trystan felt his face redden. He could guess what this was about. Who had told him? His mother?

Then he heard the murmur of the inquisitive company. "Arthur, lower your voice."

"No!" he retorted as defiantly as his mother would. "Is it true?"

Rosamunde leaned slightly forward and sweetly hissed, "Trystan, are you going to let this bastard address you in this insolent fashion?"

Although the lad did not so much as move a muscle of his face, Trystan saw the flicker of pain in his eyes. Lady Rosamunde didn't know that although Arthur usually spoke Welsh, he knew French, too, as a person of noble birth should.

"Well, are you?" Rosamunde persisted before he could suggest she use more tact.

Then Arthur proved he was indeed his mother's son, for he turned to the lady with an expression of absolute scorn and said clearly, loudly and in her own language, "You're a bitch."

"Arthur!" Trystan cried, jumping to his feet as

Lady Rosamunde flushed. "You will come with me! Excuse me, my lady."

"With very great pleasure," she replied disdainfully.

Trystan took hold of the boy's arm and marched him from the hall. He led him to a fairly secluded corner of the inner ward before coming to a halt.

"Arthur, you should not have called her that!" he declared, looking down at the obviously unrepentant boy.

"She shouldn't have called me a bastard! She had no right to call me that!"

"But you are a bastard, Arthur," he pointed out gently, wishing he did not have to be the one to drive this point home. "Your father and your mother did not marry, and that makes you one.

"To the Welsh the legalities are not so important," he explained, "but to the Normans, they are. I am afraid this will not be the last time this word will be used to describe you, either to your face or behind your back."

His heart ached to see the look in the boy's eyes, for he knew that if Mair bore him a son, one day that pain and dismay would be in his child's eyes, too.

"Trefor is a bastard," he continued. "So is Dylan, your father. So was my father. So is Uricn Fitzroy."

"My father?"

"Aye. Your grandfather and grandmother were not married." In truth, Arthur's grandfather had callously seduced a maidservant, but Arthur did not need to know that now. "And Fitzroy doesn't even know who his father was."

He knelt down so that he was eye-to-eye with Arthur. "Whether or not your parents were married is not as important as how you behave, Arthur. Remember that. If you have honesty and honor, no one can take them away from you, no matter what they call you."

Arthur nodded slowly.

"It is not honorable to call a lady that word, even if she has hurt you, and an honorable man would apologize."

Oh, how like his mother's eyes were Arthur's when Trystan said that! There was no mistaking the flash of fiery anger. "I won't! She's mean and horrible and I won't apologize!"

"You would be apologizing for the *word,* Arthur," Trystan said significantly, and he saw that the boy grasped his meaning.

"Well, and what are you two doing here looking like you're planning a war?" Mair asked merrily as she approached them. "I've been waiting for you to eat a long time, Arthur. Have you been here all this time?"

As his heart ached with longing at the sight of

her, Trystan straightened and marveled that she
could seem so pleasant, after all that had passed.

But then, that had always been Mair's way.

"Trystan's making me apologize," Arthur
grumbled.

She frowned with puzzlement. "To him? What
for?"

"To that Lady Rosamunde. Because I called her
a bitch."

"Arthur!"

He straightened his shoulders. "She called me a
bastard," he muttered defensively.

Despite his defiant stance, he colored with
shame, while Mair's entire body stiffened.

"Mair, she's a Norman," Trystan began placatingly.

Ignoring him, Mair turned to her son. "Arthur,
go home," she said evenly. "I'll be back soon."

"I don't have to apologize?"

"No."

"*He* said I should," Arthur replied, nodding at
Trystan. "He said it was the honorable thing to
do."

Then Mair looked at Trystan. God's wounds,
how she looked—as if she wanted to strike him
dead. "You want him to apologize for giving her
back what she gave?"

While Trystan sympathized with her protective

reaction, he did believe he was in the right. "If he is gallant, he will."

"Arthur, home, you, and eat," she said to her son. "I'll be back shortly."

After flashing a smile of obvious relief and a little triumph, Arthur scampered off. Meanwhile, Mair turned on her heel and headed toward the hall.

"Mair, what are you—?"

"I am going to suggest to that woman that she not call my son a bastard ever again."

"I will see that she doesn't," Trystan vowed as he hurried after her, "and I do think Arthur should apologize for using that word."

Mair halted and slowly wheeled around, glaring at him with her fiercely angry eyes. "She made my son feel ashamed for something that was not his fault. I will not have him apologize for his answer to that."

"Mair, he is the son of a baron and therefore, he must be chival—"

By the time he fell silent, she was nose-to-nose with him. "I know who his father is," she said through clenched teeth, "and I will not have my son grovel before her like he is a rush for her to step on."

"Mair, please!" he said. "I know it was not kind—"

"Kind?" she cried scornfully. "Oh, I think it

was exactly the kind of thing she can be expected to say!'' Her eyes narrowed. ''If I bear your child, will you stand by and let her hurt him that way, too? Will you make him apologize when she forces him to see how the Normans think of him—an opinion based not on his merit, but only on his birth? *Anwyl,* how chivalrous is *that?*''

She did not wait for his answer, even if he could have made one, before she whirled around and continued on her way.

Chapter Twelve

Mair strode into the hall. Her stormy gaze swept over the baron, Dylan and Baron DeLanyea's other guests who were removing their cloaks. With quick perception, she realized Sir Edward was among them.

Then she saw the Lady Rosamunde, who was seated at a small table with a chessboard. Surprisingly, Ivor stood beside her, leaning down as if attending to every utterance from her rosy lips.

Was there no man who could not see that woman for the cruel creature she was?

"Lady Rosamunde," she called out as she strode toward them, not paying the slightest jot of attention to the others gathered there, her voice like the clarion call of a hunting horn.

The Norman woman started and stared incredulously as Mair approached. Mair did not seem to notice when Trystan entered the hall, even though he called her name.

Lady Rosamunde ran a disdainful gaze over the alewife as she halted beside the table, just as her son had done.

Ivor moved back behind the lady's chair.

"What do you want?" Lady Rosamunde demanded coolly.

Mair's lips turned up in a smile.

Ivor stepped protectively closer to Lady Rosamunde. His expression wary, Dylan started toward them, until the baron held him back. He whispered to one of the servants to fetch his wife, at once.

"You upset my son," Mair said, her flashing, hostile brown eyes on Lady Rosamunde.

Trystan started to speak, but Lady Rosamunde ignored him, too, as she replied.

"You should teach him better manners," she said, likewise keeping her cool gaze on Mair. "I also suggest he wash occasionally."

"Mair, I think you should go," Trystan quickly interjected. "This is not the time or "

"Not until I tell this *bitch* a thing or two."

Lady Rosamunde turned her smug blue eyes toward her betrothed. "Sir Trystan, please get your whore out of my sight."

The hall erupted with a collective gasp of shock. Trystan flushed, Ivor stared at the floor, Lady

Rosamunde smiled with more than a hint of triumph, and Mair stood as still as a stone.

But only for the blink of an eye. "I am not a whore," she said firmly, "although you are still a bitch."

Apparently not a whit disturbed, Lady Rosamunde waved her hand dismissively. "His lover, then. His lover who is going to bear yet another bastard."

"God's wounds!" the baron murmured as he started forward, while Sir Edward looked utterly stunned.

"Trystan, is this true?" his father demanded.

"Emryss!" Lady Roanna addressed her husband from the entrance to the kitchen where she had been supervising the evening meal. She came toward them with calm grace. "As I believe Trystan started to say, this is no place to discuss such things."

"Aye, aye, you're right," the baron agreed. "Trystan, Mair, Lady Rosamunde, Sir Edward, please come to my solar and we shall get to the bottom of this."

"I won't be in the same room with that woman," Mair declared. She faced the baron squarely. "What she says is true. Trystan and I have been together, and while I cannot be completely sure, it is quite possible I'm having his baby. I ask nothing of him for myself, or of you,

Baron, because of that—but when the time comes, my son should have his due.''

Her lip curling with disdain, her gaze darted to Lady Rosamunde. "And I am *proud* to bear his child, in wedlock or out of it!"

Then she strode from the hall, her head high and her shoulders back, as regal as any queen.

"Anwyl!" Dylan muttered as he stopped watching Mair to stare at his cousin. "I've never seen Mair this angry!"

"Shut your mouth, Dylan," Trystan growled.

He looked at Rosamunde. She was flushed, and she stared down at the floor, no doubt humiliated and upset.

Was she upset enough to break their betrothal?

Then he noticed Ivor, who was regarding him with a murderous expression.

"This is no place to be speaking of these things!" Lady Roanna repeated firmly. "Come, Lady Rosamunde, Sir Edward, we shall go to the solar, where hopefully cooler heads will prevail. Trystan, go to your chamber. We will hear what you have to say later. Dylan, you sit in the baron's place."

When Lady Roanna used that tone of voice, there was not a person in Craig Fawr who would not obey. Dylan gravely went to sit at the head of the table, Trystan marched off like a man being led to his execution, and Sir Edward and his daughter followed the baron and his wife to the solar.

The moment the door to the solar closed behind the group, Sir Edward spoke, and with most unexpected calm. "Let us all be calm. Trystan is a young man. Such things are to be expected. I do not hold it against him."

"That's very generous of you," the baron replied with the tiniest hint of mockery. "However, I think it is more important to hear what Lady Rosamunde has to say."

"I am curious to know, Baron, why isn't Trystan here?" she inquired.

The baron gave her a look that was both concerned and suspicious. "I thought you might not want to be around him at present. That would be understandable."

"How kind, Baron," she said with a sweetly sorrowful smile. "However, I agree with my father. Your son is a young man, and it is only a foolish woman who believes young men can be celibate. I am not a foolish woman."

"Then you still wish to marry my son?"

"Of course!" Her sweet smile grew. "And the marriage agreement is signed, is it not? I do not want to break it, and neither should you, for it will go hard against you if you do."

The baron's eyes widened, but his wife did not look at all surprised.

"I do not think I need to be more specific as to the punishment my father and his friends could convince the king and other important men at court to exact, as well as men with whom you do business, if we so choose. Not directly, of course, and naturally I would rather not—but I will if I must."

The baron looked at Sir Edward, who was regarding his daughter with awe, and unmitigated pleasure. "You agree with what she says?" he asked. "You would threaten us?"

"If we must," Rosamunde answered for him.

"My husband addressed your father," Lady Roanna said, her serene chastisement nevertheless making Rosamunde blush.

"The agreement has been signed," Sir Edward replied warily. "It…it cannot be broken now without scandal and shame. Surely you don't want that."

Rosamunde turned her cold blue eyes and even colder smile toward the baron's wife. "You, of all people, my lady, should recall well how people will talk and rumors will fly. How many years was it before the court ceased speaking of your rape at this man's hands?"

"I never raped my wife!" the baron cried, aghast.

"So you say," the young woman continued, her steadfast gaze still on the man's unresponsive spouse, "but there were stories. Of course, it was also said Dylan DeLanyea's father raped her, too."

"She was never raped!"

"Oh, dear. Isn't gossip terrible?" Lady Rosamunde's expression grew as hard as the stones of the castle. "Be that as it may, I will not be subjected to any gossip. Your son asked for my hand in marriage, and I consented. The marriage terms have been agreed upon, and the contract signed. If he tries to break it now, you will pay dearly, in money and more. Are you willing to have that happen?"

"For my son's happiness, I would gladly risk much more," Lady Roanna said with the majesty of an empress. "Now I have your measure, my young lady. Come, Emryss, let us talk to Trystan."

Her lip curled ever so slightly into a scornful smile. "And counsel him to think no more of marrying this bitch."

"God's wounds, Trystan! You can't marry that woman!" his father growled as he regarded his son incredulously. "Her threats don't trouble us nearly as much as you marrying her would!"

Trystan's gaze shifted from his father to his mother and back again. They had told him of Rosamunde's threat, and that, in their opinion, he should break the marriage contract.

Yet he would not. He could well believe that

Rosamunde would make good her warning, and more. His father was well-known and powerful here in the borderlands between Wales and England, and he had several Norman friends, but when it came to power where it meant the most—at court—that was not so certain. It was quite possible that if Rosamunde's family and friends became their enemy, the results could be disastrous.

And as Dylan had said, what affected them, affected him. If his father's friends chose to stand with him, they could suffer, too.

Even then, he knew, he might risk all that, if Mair had said she loved him enough to marry.

But she had not. She had made love to him as she had all her other lovers, and she was bearing a child just as she had Dylan's; more than that, she was not willing to give.

Why not marry Rosamunde, therefore, and prevent trouble? The marriage could yet provide all the advantages he had originally thought so important.

He would never love her, of course. Indeed, he could never love her after all that had passed, but he had made a promise, and he would keep it. He himself had thrown away his chance for true happiness in favor of worldly gain when he had asked her to be his wife, and no one but he should suffer for it.

"I will not break the contract," he repeated.

"But Trystan, she's a cold-hearted—"

"Perhaps," he interrupted. "How can you expect her to be warm and loving after what she has learned about her betrothed? Besides, I would rather she behave bravely and maintain her rights than sob and rant and rave."

He had to make them believe he still wanted Rosamunde, or they would break the contract whether he agreed or not. "Mam, she knows her rights, that's all. I was in the wrong, not her. I shouldn't have made love with Mair, not when I was courting her. That was wrong and shameful."

"So now you must suffer for it by marrying Rosamunde?"

His mother might make others think her serene with that expression but in the depths of her eyes there was another emotion Trystan could see that added to his pain: disappointment.

"No!" he insisted. "I want to marry her. If I didn't, I wouldn't have asked her in the first place."

"But she's—"

"She's the woman I want, Da."

"You weren't in the solar with her standing there like the coldest, most vicious—"

"Da! Didn't you hear me? She's the woman I'm going to marry. Please don't insult her."

"Trystan," Lady Roanna said, "why did you make love with Mair?"

He strode toward the window and looked out at the tower for a moment, then slowly turned back. "Because I could."

He saw shock and disillusionment and frustration on his father's face. All his life he had tried to live up to the standards his father and brother and cousin had set. He had never thought he could fail so completely, and by his own act.

But show his anguish he would not, because he was a DeLanyea.

And he did not dare to even glance at his mother.

"I see," he heard her say. "Then we will say no more against this marriage, or her."

"But—" the baron protested.

"Emryss, we shall say no more. The marriage will take place as planned, because it is what Trystan wants. Good night, Trystan."

His father left without another word, following his wife from the chamber and closing the door behind him.

When they had gone, Trystan turned back to stare out the window, seeing nothing but the blackness of the night sky.

And the hopelessness of the future he had made for himself.

* * *

"Is my da really a bastard?" Arthur asked eagerly, looking up from his trencher of stew the moment Mair appeared in the door.

She wearily closed the door, then forced herself to smile when she looked at him. "Yes."

"And the baron?"

"Yes."

"Fitzroy, too?" Arthur continued with awe.

It was no secret that Arthur, like most people, considered Fitzroy without peer when it came to the arts of war.

"Yes."

"And the king?"

Mair's smile became genuine at that fervent question. "No, Arthur, the king is not."

The lad shook his head, obviously pitying the sovereign for the legality of his birth.

Whatever Trystan had said, he had managed to take the sting out of Lady Rosamunde's words, and for that, Mair was grateful.

"Arthur, I have to talk to you about something important," she said, coming to sit beside him on the bench.

"I'll apologize if I have to," he replied with determined courage.

"No, you don't have to. This isn't about Lady Rosamunde."

She took a deep breath. "I may be having a baby, and if I am, Sir Trystan is the father."

"Not that Ivor?"

"No, not that Ivor."

Arthur grinned. "Good! I like him a lot better than Ivor."

Mair supposed she should be glad he wasn't upset.

Then Arthur grew pensive. "Is Trystan still going to marry that Lady Rosamunde, or you?"

"Lady Rosamunde."

"The new baby will be a bastard, too!"

It seemed Trystan had given her son rather too much comfort over his illegitimacy. "Yes, he will."

"He?"

"Angharad thinks it is a boy."

Arthur laughed. "Trefor doesn't have any brothers or sisters!" he cried triumphantly. "I never thought of that before!"

"Arthur, don't cast that up to him! That would be cruel, and have you not learned how that kind of cruelty can hurt?"

Her son stopped grinning. "What if he says something mean to me?"

Considering what she herself had just done, she could hardly tell him to keep silent. Instead, she rose and busied herself clearing the table.

"What if he says something mean to me?" Arthur persisted.

"He will not be here after next month, so I don't think you need to worry about it."

"I wish Trystan wasn't marrying that Norman," Arthur said as he helped her. "She's nasty."

"She's very beautiful and her family are very important."

"Is that why he isn't marrying you?"

"No, Arthur. I wouldn't marry him."

"Why not?"

"Because that is my business, my son, and not yours. When you're older, I'll try to explain."

Arthur looked up at her. "I think you're a lot prettier than she is, Mam."

Mair smiled tenderly. "Thank you, Arthur." She reached out and ruffled his dark hair, then sighed. "How I'm going to miss you when you go to Fitzroy!"

Suddenly Arthur embraced her fiercely. "I'll miss you, too, Mam." He raised his boyish eyes to look at her. "But when I come back, I'll be a squire. And when I'm a knight, I'll be the best knight in the land, and win lots of tournaments and battles and rewards and honors. I'll get a big castle, and then you'll come live with me, and we'll never be apart ever any more. I'll make you proud of me, Mam, I swear!"

Mair held him all the tighter. "I am already proud of you, my son."

A fortnight later, Baron Emryss DeLanyea sat in the solar of Beaufort, Dylan's castle. Dylan sat on his left, and the baron's eldest son, grim, gray-eyed Griffydd, sat on his right. They were the only people there, for this was a family council.

"Is there nothing we can do?" Dylan demanded, looking anxiously from his uncle to his cousin.

"He is adamant that he will marry her," the baron replied.

"Perhaps he does care for her, then," Griffydd noted.

"If he does, he is a fool!" Dylan cried. "I never saw a woman more likely to make a husband miserable—and that was before we heard of her threats."

"Did you mention your concerns to Trystan?"

"Good God, no. You can guess how he would have responded. He thought he was in love with her."

"And it could be he *is* in love with her," Griffydd answered calmly.

"He might have believed he was at one time," the baron said to his son, "but you didn't see him that night in his chamber. Although he insists upon marrying the woman, he doesn't love her. Indeed, I don't think he feels anything for her at all."

"Then stop the marriage."

The baron regarded Dylan patiently. "I gave him the opportunity to refuse to proceed, and he said he wanted to marry her. How can I go against his wishes now without humiliating him? I dare not, lest I make things worse.''

"Surely you don't fear Sir Edward and his cronies?" Dylan asked incredulously.

"No," the baron replied sternly. "I fear losing my son."

"What does my mother say?"

The baron gave his eldest son a wry look. "Not surprisingly, she counsels patience."

"She is wise. If we all try to make Trystan change his mind, though it be for his own good, he will not take it kindly."

"But—"

Griffydd fastened his shrewd gaze onto his cousin. "You wouldn't listen to any of us under similar circumstances, or have you already forgotten?"

"That was different. I loved Genevieve. I just didn't know it."

"And it could be we are wrong about Trystan's feelings. I don't want to believe my brother would be so stubbornly stupid."

"We DeLanyeas are all stubborn," the baron observed. "It's in the blood." He rose and started to pace, limping.

"What about Mair?" Dylan demanded. "Is he going to abandon her?"

"You are a fine one to talk about abandoning Mair," Griffydd remarked.

"She didn't love me, and I didn't love her."

"Trystan implied that he doesn't love her," the baron said.

"Then he *is* a fool! God's wounds, I saw the way he looked at her. It was like the way he looked at Genevieve when he claimed to love her, only worse."

"He looked worse?"

"Don't be dim, Griffydd. You know what I mean. More in love. More passionate. I noticed the difference when I came for Arthur. They must have already made love by then."

"That doesn't mean he loves her enough to marry her. You should know all about that," Griffydd replied.

"That was different. Oh, for the sake of all the saints, it was different between Mair and me. I know it, she knows it, and unless he's blind as a bat, Trystan knows it, too. Mair never looked at me the way she does him, try as she might to hide it. If only the boy didn't have so much ambition!"

"You think he would marry for ambition?"

"What else, if he weds that Norman?"

"Because he made a promise and now, for honor's sake, will not break it," the baron growled. "God's wounds, I fear I talked too much of honor when you were all growing up. You would all of you sacrifice honor to happiness, I think."

"Not I," Dylan hastened to say.

The baron paused. "That isn't what I thought when you insisted upon marrying your wife."

Dylan colored. "I told you, I loved her."

"We are here because of Trystan's marriage," Griffydd reminded them. He looked at the baron. "Do you honestly believe he does not love this woman, and that she will not be a fit wife for him?"

"Yes, I do."

"Then what would you have us do? Try to talk him out of it? As you say, we DeLanyeas are stubborn. I do not think that would work."

The baron shook his head. "I wish you were not always so accurate in your reasoning, my son. Still, you get it from your mother, and she thinks such a course of action would be futile, too."

"So what does Lady Roanna say we should do?" Dylan demanded impatiently.

"Come to his wedding and smile when you stand by his side." The baron's expression grew cold and grim. "If he must wed this woman, the least we can do is show her family and friends—"

"That if there is any trouble to come, he will not be alone," Griffydd finished, rising and meeting his father's gaze.

"Aye," the baron said firmly. "And to let Trystan know it, too."

Chapter Thirteen

Two days before the wedding of Sir Trystan DeLanyea and Lady Rosamunde D'Heureux, Mair drove her wagon full of barrels of ale, mead and *braggot* into the courtyard of Craig Fawr. That was not an easy thing to do, for it was already crowded with wedding guests and their entourages.

Mair waved at Arthur and Trefor, who had come early that morning and now stood on the wall walk waiting to see their father and his party arrive. They waved back briefly, then returned to scrutinizing the arrivals.

Mair maneuvered her cart as close to the kitchen as she could, pulled her horse to a halt and looked around for a familiar servant to help her unload the barrels.

"Well, well, well, what have we here?" a languid, male Norman voice asked slyly.

She glanced over her shoulder to see a group of

young men lounging by the stable entrance. One of them, well-dressed and coiffed in the Norman fashion, and obviously the leader, pushed himself from the wall and sauntered toward her wagon, his similarly attired fellows following along behind.

Mair heaved a sigh as she jumped nimbly to the ground. No doubt they would like to believe they resembled a lean and hungry pack of fierce wolves, and that she should be impressed with them, if not afraid.

The Norman fools. To her, they were more like ducklings waddling after their mother.

"See how this Welsh wench hurries down to meet me?" the stranger said with a laugh. "For the first time since I came to the borderlands I regret I cannot speak Welsh."

With a mocking smile on her face, Mair continued to watch them approach.

"See how she smiles? And did you see what lovely legs she has?" he said, addressing his companions as if she were not even there. "A man would pay well to get between them."

"A man would have to be a man to get between them, not an overdressed popinjay," Mair observed in their tongue.

As his friends exchanged amused glances, the leader colored slightly. "Watch your tongue, wench, or I'll—"

"Or you'll what?" Trystan demanded as he appeared at the door of the stable and made his way toward them.

Mair had not seen him since the confrontation with Rosamunde and her heart ached at the sight of him.

It was not just her own hopeless longing that filled her with anguish, but the change that had come over him. It was as if he had aged ten years. His eyes were as hard as slate and cold as iron. His face had grown thinner, as if he had been seriously ill and unable to eat, yet she had heard no word of an illness.

"Who are you?" the Norman demanded haughtily.

"The bridegroom."

The man glanced at his companions, then bowed with a flourish. "I am Lady Rosamunde's cousin, Sir Cecil D'Heureux and honored to make your acquaintance, Sir Trystan. I am sorry if I have caused offense."

"Welcome to Craig Fawr, and you should be asking Mair's pardon, not mine, for your rudeness."

Mair had never heard him sound so much like his father, when his father was angry.

"But she is nothing more than—"

"Do you have difficulty hearing, Sir Cecil?"

Sir Cecil ran a cursory glance over the wagon before looking again at Mair. Then understanding dawned in his eyes. "Ah, this is the alewife of whom I have heard."

"What have you heard?" Mair demanded.

"Why, that your…ale…is the best to be had in all of Wales."

Sir Cecil's companions exchanged amused and insolent glances.

Mair crossed her arms over her chest as Sir Cecil smiled sardonically and made a very small bow in her direction. "I beg your pardon. I shall look forward to tasting your wares."

Trystan's hand went to his sword.

Mair felt a hint of panic. There was no need for drawn swords. She had been dealing with impertinent, insolent rogues for years, and Trystan should know that. She didn't need him to be her gallant protector, especially when his potential opponent was his betrothed's relation.

She would find another way to end this.

Mair started to laugh, a deep, throaty gurgling noise.

Trystan watched grimly as she all but danced toward the arrogant Norman, her hands on her slender hips, her eyes merry.

He anxiously searched for any sign that she might be with child. Unfortunately, her everyday gown was as loosely belted and bloused as always, so she could be months gone and he could still not be sure.

"Oh, Sir Cecil, how flattered I am to think you could care!" she cried in the teasing tone she used to use with him. "To think that I may have your good opinion! Oh, how shall I survive the delight!"

Sir Cecil stared at her incredulously while around the courtyard, the inhabitants of Craig Fawr who had been surreptitiously watching them started to laugh.

When the Norman realized they were laughing at him, he scowled darkly. "I think that woman's possessed."

"Oh, aye, I am," she retorted gaily, clasping her hands together like a lovesick maiden. "By a hopeless passion for attractive, well-dressed Normans, even ones who make rude remarks."

Sir Cecil stopped scowling. Then, to Trystan's surprise and inward dismay, he began to smile with amused approval.

"Mair, that's enough," Trystan snapped. "If you would care to join me in the hall, Sir Cecil, I will have refreshments brought."

"By her?" he asked, nodding at Mair.

"Alas, Sir Cecil, I am not a serving wench."

Instead of looking annoyed at her bold retort, his approving smile grew.

"If you fine gentlemen will excuse me, I have ale to deliver."

"By all means do not let me keep such a delightful creature from her duty,'' Sir Cecil replied, oblivious to the black look Trystan was giving him.

A look that had disappeared by the time Sir Cecil had stopped watching Mair as she went into the kitchen, then faced his host's son.

''Although I would never upset the bride, I can well understand how a man would be tempted to have that wench for a mistress,'' Sir Cecil remarked in the tone of one man of the world to another.

''She is not my mistress,'' Trystan growled before he turned on his heel and led the way toward the hall, loathing Sir Cecil and his ilk to the marrow of his bones.

It did not help that he was going to have to associate with his bride's relatives in the years to come.

Nor could he take any comfort from coming to Mair's aid, for he knew full well she could have managed without him. Indeed, he rather wished he had not interfered, for then he would not have had to look at Mair.

The sight of her and the longing she inspired was almost too much to bear.

And yet that agony had not been enough to keep him away from her the moment he had heard her voice.

Some time later, her ale safely delivered to the baron's storehouse, Mair sat in the large, comfortable and bustling kitchen of the castle, partaking of a little refreshment. Dylan had arrived and she lingered while Arthur and Trefor visited with their father. Later they would ride home with her in her cart.

"So I thought the cask might start leaking. What would I do if I did?" Mair asked rhetorically as the servants paid no heed to their tasks to listen to her.

She brandished her bread philosophically. "And then the answer came to me! I would mark it for Sir Edward! It would be empty before anybody noticed the leak!"

As the servants chortled, they suddenly realized Trystan was standing in the door leading to the hall. They fell silent and quickly went back to work.

"Ah, Sir Trystan," Mair said evenly.

She smiled genially as she rose, set down the remains of the bread and brushed the crumbs from her bodice. That simple action nearly drove him mad with a desire that he could hardly suppress.

But that he must.

"Where are your charming Norman friends?" she inquired.

"Will you come with me to my mother's garden?"

"Whatever will your bride say to that?"

Trystan tried to ignore the servants' curious, if surreptitious, glances. "If you would rather speak in the midst of so many people, so be it."

"I can't think of a single thing you could have to say to me that could not be shouted from the wall walk."

He flushed. "I have no desire to do anything on the wall walk."

"Neither have I."

"I would rather speak to you alone," he persisted, looking at her intently.

Her gaze faltered for a moment.

"Well, we have been alone before, so why not again?" she declared as if he were nothing at all to her, and never had been. "Off to the garden, then."

With an airy wave to the servants, she sauntered out of the room while Trystan followed behind like some kind of lap dog.

"So, here we are, alone in the garden," Mair announced as she turned to face him after going through the gate. "And what a nice bit of gossip you've given your father's servants."

"Are they going to have more to gossip about soon? Are you with child?"

Looking around at the dead roses, she shrugged her slender shoulders in a gesture that was frustratingly noncommittal.

"This is not a game to me, Mair."

"I should hope not. What would you call it? Standing in a garden? Not a lot of fun, that."

"Mair!" he cried, and the hint of anguished tension in his voice was enough to make her look at him with genuine concern. "Mair, I have to know. *Are you with child?*"

Her mask of flippant indifference slipped. "Yes."

"For certain?"

"As certain as it is possible to be."

His shoulders slumped. "Oh, God's wounds, I'm sorry, Mair."

She approached him slowly, warily, as if he were a wild animal who might make a sudden, unexpected move. "Sorry?"

"For making love with you. For putting you in this untenable position. For making it possible for men like Sir Cecil and his friends to talk to you in that disgusting way."

Her brown eyes softened with tender sympathy. "I'm not, Trystan. I wasn't sorry for making love with you when I did it, and I'm not sorry now."

She gently took his face between her palms, smiling at him lovingly. "Listen to me, Trystan, and listen well. I am *glad* for what we did. I am happy beyond words to be having another child. I don't expect you to be my great protector. I have managed by myself for long before this, and can continue to do so."

With a ragged, weary sigh, he turned his head to press a kiss on her palm.

She snatched her hands away as if his lips were on fire. "And as for Sir Cecil—he's a fool, and that is not your fault."

She gave him one of her mischievous, sidelong glances. "Besides, I know another young man who used to insult me all the time, although not like that."

"I'm sorry for all the harsh and hasty things I've ever said to you, Mair. I have been a pigheaded fool, just like Sir Cecil."

Something flickered deep in her eyes. "Oh, no, Trystan, you were never like him. I wouldn't have—" She hesitated. "I wouldn't have let you touch me if you were."

"How charming," Lady Rosamunde declared from the gate of the garden.

She came inside, a cool smile on her lovely face, the breeze fluttering her veil, her hips swaying. "I've been searching for the bridegroom and here he is, and not alone. Really, Trystan, if you want to have your little assignations with this wench you will have to be more subtle."

"We weren't having any assignation," Mair retorted, running a scornful gaze over Rosamunde.

"I daresay you don't even know what that means."

"I can guess."

"Trystan, tell this woman to go back to her ale."

Regarding Rosamunde steadily, Trystan addressed Mair evenly. "Please go now, Mair, and leave me with my beautiful bride."

Mair glanced from him to the triumphant Norman woman. "Gladly."

"Then be gone," Rosamunde suggested.

Mair gave her a scornful look before she spoke to Trystan, who finally looked at her. "God be with you, Trystan."

"God be with you, Mair, and may happiness come to you."

She nodded, her lips smiling and her eyes grim, before she left Rosamunde the victor on the field.

"I mean what I say, Trystan," Rosamunde declared, strolling closer to the man she commanded. "If you must sport with whores, I would rather you didn't do so in so obvious a fashion."

Trystan stayed silent as he watched Mair leave. Then he looked at his Norman bride and quietly inquired, "Rosamunde, do you value your life?"

She gave him an incredulous look. "What?"

He approached her slowly, like a large cat drawing near an unsuspecting prey. As she saw the look in his eyes, Rosamunde paled.

"If you value your life, you will never again call Mair a whore, or any other disparaging name. You

will never insult either her, or the child she bears
me—or God help me, you will be sorry.''

"You...you savage! How dare you threaten
me—and for that—'' Wisely, she hesitated. "That
woman.''

He smiled slowly. "Apparently you did not
think it amiss to threaten me and my family, so
why should I not threaten you?''

Rosamunde started to back away. "What...what
would you do?'' she whispered, arrogance replaced
by awe and dread.

"I do not think you should be anxious to find
out.''

She made no reply before she turned and fled.

Leaving Trystan alone with his thoughts. And
his regrets.

Fighting the exhaustion that came from main-
taining an outwardly cheerful attitude so at odds
with her inner turmoil, Mair walked through the
courtyard toward the stable. She would get her
horse ready for the journey home by herself, glad
that all the grooms and stable hands were in the
hall waiting for the evening meal.

Breathing in the scent of straw and horse and
leather, she went to the stall where her horse stood
munching on some oats. Cooing softly, she ran her
hand over his firm hindquarters, which quivered at
her touch. He turned his head to regard her.

"Even you have taken to looking at me like I'm a bit mad, is it?" she whispered with a weary chuckle. "Maybe I am. Mad for love. Me!" she finished incredulously.

Her horse went back to his oats.

Deciding she could wait a bit before fetching the harness since she couldn't be sure when Arthur would come, and most definitely sure she would not venture into the hall to find out, she leaned wearily against a post. She closed her eyes and tried to will away the tears that threatened to come.

"Mair?"

With a choking gasp, she whirled around to see Dylan staring at her with frank curiosity.

"Dylan!" she cried, the word almost a croak. She cleared her throat. "*Anwyl,* it's dusty in here! Did you bring Arthur?" she asked, looking past him. "Where is he?"

"He and Trefor are still helping Genevieve unpack my baggage."

"And being more hindrance than help to her, I'm sure."

"She enjoys their company."

"And they like poking about your things."

He crossed the floor toward her. "Mair, are you having Trystan's child?"

"I think I am going to have to stand on the battlements and make an announcement or I shall be pestered with questions all the time."

"Are you?"

She decided there was no point to prevaricating. "Yes, I am. In the late spring, or thereabouts."

"How does he feel about it?"

"How should he feel?"

"That's not what I'm asking."

"How did you feel when I told you I was having your baby?"

"You know how I felt. I was thrilled."

"You were not about to be married to somebody else."

"I hope he's being honorable about it."

"He's Trystan, so of course he is."

Dylan's dark-eyed scrutiny grew even more intense. "Thank God for that."

"Yes, thank God for that," she agreed. "Now, if that is all you want to ask me—"

"What do you think of Rosamunde?"

"What does it matter what I think?"

"Surely you don't want Trystan to marry her?"

"It's not for me to say."

"He's supposed to be marrying you."

"You've been talking to Angharad again, haven't you?"

Dylan took her hands in his and gazed into her eyes as if he could transfix her with a look, as indeed Dylan could when he stared like that. "I want you to answer me honestly, Mair. Do you love him?"

"If I bear his child, I must have loved him, mustn't I?"

Dylan frowned with frustration. "Mair, please be serious. I think he loves you as much as a man can love a woman."

"Oh, and you are a seer, too, like Angharad?"

"I am a man in love myself, so I know what to look for. Now I need to know if *you* love *him*."

"Don't tell me you are jealous?" She tried to laugh scornfully and instead produced something that sounded horrible. "No, I'm not."

"Are you jealous of Lady Rosamunde?"

"No."

"Not of her for herself, I mean. Because Trystan is going to marry her."

"If he wants her, he can have her."

"I don't think he does want her. Not anymore. Not after being with you."

Mair looked away, then sniffed derisively and raised her brave brown eyes to look at him. "*Anwyl,* Dylan, you know I'm not that wonderful a lover, and I'm certainly not so vain as to believe that after making love with me, Trystan is unable to feel desire for any other woman."

Dylan regarded her gravely. "Vanity has nothing to do with it. I think he loves you very much."

This time, Mair couldn't meet his steadfast gaze. She took a deep breath before she spoke. "Then he should get over it. My leaving here should help.''

''Leaving? Where are you going?''

''I'll sell the brewery and move to Bridgeford Wells, to be near Arthur while he trains.''

''But your home is here.''

''My ale will sell wherever I am, I think.''

''Arthur might do better if you are not nearby.''

She gave him a look that told him she could not be dissuaded. ''He will do well wherever I am. I have made up my mind, Dylan. I am going to Bridgeford Wells.''

''To get away from Trystan.''

''Because I want to be nearer Arthur.''

''Are you trying to convince *me* that you do not love Trystan—or yourself? If so, I think you are failing on both counts. The truth now, Mair. I have to know. Do you love him?''

''He should marry Lady Rosamunde. He deserves a wife who can bring him what he wants.''

''What is it that he wants?''

''He wants no more than he deserves, to be a great and respected lord. He can be, if he marries well.''

''But to marry only for ambition, and to one like that, will soon make him miserable. I know enough of Trystan to know that, even if he does not. I think you must not love him, either, if you would allow him to suffer in such a way.''

"Dylan, shut your mouth and go away!" she cried, hurrying away from him and his questions and his eyes and his words to the far corner of the stable, which was deep in shadow.

Dylan followed after, a sympathetic, yet equally determined, look on his face. "You *do* love him. I knew it!"

She spun on her heel to face him. "It doesn't matter what I feel," she said vehemently. "It is what Trystan wants that is important."

She drew in a ragged sigh. "It will be enough that he cared for me once, at least a little, and that I have his child. Now say no more of Trystan to me, Dylan. Please, if you have any mercy in you, say no more of him!"

She put her head in her hands and, despite her pride and her resolution, started to weep with all the fierce passion of her nature.

Dylan gently took her in his arms. "Hush, Mair, hush," he crooned as he held her comfortingly. "It shall be as you wish. I will say no more about it."

That is what he said.

But Mair could not see the look in his eyes as he said it.

"I tell you, Angharad, something must be done!" Dylan declared as he smashed his fist on the table in her house.

He had brought their son home, and lingered to

complain while Trefor went to the brook to fetch some water.

"The baron—?"

"Says we must not interfere, even now, but that's not right!"

"Why do you say that?" Angharad asked as she glanced up from her spinning.

"Because they love each other so much!"

"If that were true, Trystan wouldn't be marrying Lady Rosamunde, would he?" Angharad inquired as she stopped spinning. "And Mair would not be going away."

"I don't think he knows how Mair feels about him, and Mair will do what she thinks right, no matter how it hurts her. *Anwyl,* she should have been a warrior, her, for a more resolute face I never saw on any man."

"You seem very certain of their feelings for one another," Angharad noted as she put away her spindle.

"I am!"

"How can you be? Did they confide in you?"

Mindful of Mair's dismay, Dylan kept her words to himself. "It is enough that I am sure. She cares for Trystan more than she ever has for any other man, including me."

"I know how difficult an admission that must be for you to make, so I am sure you don't do so lightly."

"I don't!" he confirmed as he looked at the mother of his firstborn, a fine woman he still respected.

And, truth be told, feared a little because of her gift.

"Besides," he continued, "I would think you would agree with me. You've always said he would wed Mair, not some Norman woman."

Angharad straightened to regard her former lover steadily, and seriously. "Are you truly worried that Trystan is making a grievous mistake?"

"Yes!"

"Why would he marry if he didn't love?"

"Because he asked Rosamunde before he knew his own heart, or what she was! Because she's threatened repercussions if he doesn't! Because he's a fool!"

Dylan ran a hand through his shoulder-length hair. "My father thinks there is something amiss with Trystan, too, yet he insists we mustn't say a word to him of our misgivings. Indeed, he and Lady Roanna would have us welcome Rosamunde with open arms. She'd try to seduce me if I got my arms around her, that one!"

"You are a vain creature, Dylan DeLanyea."

"You've not seen her at a feast, or you would know I am being honest, not vain."

Angharad smiled. Then her dark eyes, that sometimes looked like the inky depths of a lake in moonlight, grew serious. "There is a way to prevent the marriage, if you are absolutely certain Trystan really doesn't want this woman for his wife."

"You've got the Sight. Aren't you sure he's asked the wrong one?"

"I only know that he's going to be happily wed and have fine, healthy sons and one daughter. I cannot call the visions to come, you know, Dylan. They come as they will."

Then she smiled. "But I have had one that I do not doubt to be true, and if you are willing to do what must be done, no man will wonder if Trystan doesn't marry Lady Rosamunde, and there will be no question of reprisals."

Chapter Fourteen

Trystan awoke the moment he felt the hand over his mouth. Struggling to sit up, he opened his eyes to find a man bending over him like the Angel of Death come to take him away, an effect aided by the shadows cast by the flickering torch he held.

After he realized it was only Dylan, he gave a smothered roar of anger and swatted at his cousin.

"Be quiet, boy!" Dylan ordered in Welsh as two other hands clamped down on his shoulders, "and then I'll take my hand away."

Trystan glared at Griffydd, who held him. Then he scanned the faces of the other men who surrounded his bed,

He was shocked to see his father standing at the foot, and Sir Cecil and his Norman friends crowded behind him. Although it was very dark, no one else carried any kind of light.

Nevertheless, it seemed as if every male wedding guest was there, with the exception of Sir Edward. They all looked as if they, too, had recently been roused from sleep, and there was a curious air of excited suspense about them, as well.

"Are you going to be quiet?"

Trystan nodded, and Dylan slowly removed his hand.

"What's the meaning of this?" Trystan demanded, albeit quietly and also in Welsh. "Are we under attack?"

"No. Get dressed and come with us," Griffydd ordered.

Trystan ignored his brother as he looked to his father. "Da, what's happening? Why are all these men here?"

"Do as Dylan says, my son," the baron replied grimly.

Taken aback by his father's resigned attitude as much as by the nocturnal intrusion and very aware that he was naked as he got out of the bed, Trystan did as he was told.

As he pulled on his breeches, he glanced anxiously at his father again. "Is somebody hurt?"

He was surprised by the sorrowful look that came to his father's resolute face. "Not yet," the baron replied quietly.

His response made Trystan more puzzled than ever. His father had never approved of vigilante activity, and Trystan could think of no crime recently committed that would require it anyway.

When Trystan was dressed, Dylan signaled his cousin to join him at the door. "Quiet now, for what we are about to do requires absolute silence."

He switched to French, and his tone changed, too, to one of festive merriment. "Come along, gentlemen."

The Normans exchanged amused glances and likewise did as they were bid. It took a few moments before Trystan realized Dylan was leading the way toward the tower housing Lady Rosamunde's bedchamber.

"What is this all about?" Trystan demanded quietly in Welsh of his cousin.

"Have you never heard of the groom's traditional visit to the bridal chamber the night before the wedding?"

"No, because there is no such tradition, as you well know," Trystan retorted.

"There should be, I'm thinking."

"I'm not sure I should give my countenance to this barbaric Welsh custom," they heard Sir Cecil mutter behind them. "Really, to visit my cousin in her bedchamber—"

Dylan laughed softly. "I told you, in Wales, the male wedding guests try to get a glimpse of the bride's body," he said in French. "It used to be with an eye to approving of her. Not anymore, of course, for the Welsh are much more civilized, thanks to the Normans.''

Although those behind could not, Trystan saw the sarcastic mockery on Dylan's face.

"Naturally, we don't ask her to take off her clothes anymore," Dylan continued. "Now we just try to sneak a glimpse of her legs."

"Why are you telling such monstrous lies?" Trystan demanded in Welsh, looking over his shoulder for his father, who surely should put a stop to this.

"Shh, we're nearly there. You don't want to wake her, do you?''

"He's not being very generous, this cousin of mine," Dylan complained to the Normans, switching again to their language. "He doesn't want anybody else to see her lovely limbs, the miser."

The men behind chuckled and exchanged amused whispers, until they were nearly at the bedchamber door.

"Gentlemen, please," Dylan cautioned them in a conspiratorial whisper. "We must be quiet, or the surprise will be spoiled."

Trystan came to a halt, his hands on his hips. He had had quite enough of this mystery. "Dylan, I don't know what this is about, or what you think you're doing—"

Somebody behind him encircled him with one

powerful arm and clapped a strong, callused hand over his mouth.

"It will all be clear soon," Griffydd muttered in Trystan's ear as he frog-marched his brother toward the chamber door.

Without a knock or word of warning, Dylan abruptly shoved it open and went inside. All the men crowded in behind, including Trystan and Griffydd.

Then they all stared dumbfounded at the sight that met their eyes.

After a moment of shocked horror, Rosamunde screamed and the captain of the guard scrambled naked from the lady's bed.

They had been in the throes of passionate lovemaking, and despite her hurried efforts to cover herself, it was all too clear that the lady was as naked as her lover.

Griffydd let go of Trystan, who stood motionless and silent.

Clutching the bedclothes to her rounded breasts, and wild-eyed, Rosamunde stared at them. Then she pointed a trembling hand at Ivor, who was frantically tying his breeches. "He attacked me! He raped me!"

His tunic in his hands, Ivor turned toward her, a horrified expression on his face.

"He did! He came into my room uninvited! He...he threw me on the bed and stripped me and nearly smothered me to death as he took his pleasure of me, although I fought and kicked—''

''Rosamunde!'' Ivor cried, letting his tunic fall to the floor unheeded. ''That's a lie! I never forced you! I love you, and you love me. I want to marry you.''

''Marry you?'' she screamed as if his declaration filled her with revulsion. ''Are you mad? Marry a captain of a guard? A Welshman with no title or noble blood?''

Wrapping the sheet around her, Rosamunde climbed from the bed.

''Cecil, you believe me, don't you?'' she pleaded as she went toward her cousin. ''You must believe me! You know I would never allow such a barbarian into my bed!''

''Rosamunde, tell them the truth,'' Ivor begged. ''As I am an honorable man, tell them I came here at your invitation.''

She glared at him, her teeth bared like a trapped animal. ''My invitation? To you, a mere soldier? Every man knows that has to be a lie. I could never love a man like you, never! You attacked me, you base, horrible savage, and you should be executed for your crime!''

''Executed?'' Ivor gasped, turning as pale as the white linen that Rosamunde held to her flushed body.

"There will be no execution," the baron declared from the back of the group of men.

"Indeed, no, there will not," Sir Cecil confirmed. "I fear, fair cousin, this does not look well for you. Where are your bruises? Your wounds? The door was unlocked. Why did you not flee? And why are your clothes not scattered upon the floor, ripped and ruined?"

With grimly sorrowful eyes, Ivor looked at Trystan, who still had not moved, and then the other DeLanyeas. "My lords, you must believe me. I didn't attack her, I came here at her behest tonight, and it is not for the first time."

"Liar!" Rosamunde screamed. She hurried to Trystan and fell on the floor at his feet. "Trystan, he attacked me! As you love me, you must believe me!"

"As your own cousin has pointed out, I see no evidence of an attack, on him or on you," Trystan replied flatly.

"You have to believe me! You have to marry me!" she pleaded, truly desperate now.

"No, he doesn't," Sir Cecil said, disgust in his patrician voice. "You disappoint me, cousin, and you shame our family. If I were you, I would contemplate retirement to a nunnery."

Rosamunde slowly got to her feet, glaring at him. Then her haughty gaze swept over all of them. "So I am a disgrace, although the man I am to marry has a whore who is going to bear him a bastard?''

"I told you if you called Mair a whore again you would regret it," Trystan said slowly and deliberately, regarding her steadily. "I will never marry you now."

"And no man here will hold you at fault for breaking the marriage contract," Sir Cecil said. "You have disgraced your good name, Rosamunde."

"That's not fair! You men can have all sorts of lovers before and after marriage, and yet a woman cannot, or else her reputation is destroyed."

"No, it isn't fair," the baron agreed with some mercy in his deep voice. "But it is the way of the world in which you Normans live. A pity it is, my lady, that you are not Welsh, for we would forgive you the lapse, if not the lie."

His visage grew stern. "I have known Ivor all his life, and he would no sooner take a woman against her will than he would kill a child, so I know you are giving false witness when you claim he did so."

She looked pleadingly at Trystan. "Please, Trystan, you must forgive me. I will never betray you after we are married. I give you my solemn vow."

"I shall forgive you for your weakness, for I have been weak, too."

She started to smile with relief, until he continued.

"But I cannot forgive your lies, and the way you spoke of the woman I love."

She started to sob, yet he continued inexorably. "The marriage agreement notwithstanding, I shall not marry you tomorrow, or any other day. Nor shall I ever speak to you again."

With that, he turned on his heel and marched out of the room, the grave Normans making way for him.

The baron looked at Ivor. "You have betrayed my trust, Ivor. Get your things and leave Craig Fawr at once."

The man nodded. "I am sorry for the trouble I have brought to your household," he said quietly, and with dignity. "Farewell, Baron."

Then, he, too, stoically left the room.

The baron turned and followed him, trailed by his nephew and his eldest son, then the others.

While Rosamunde huddled on the cold stone floor sobbing with genuine sorrow over the ruin of her scheme, and vowing to hate all men for the rest of her life.

"That was the only way to do it, Trys," Dylan said quietly as he sat in his cousin's bedchamber later that night.

The two men were alone. The baron had gone

with Sir Cecil to explain the situation to Sir Edward. Griffydd had taken it upon himself to tell Lady Roanna and the other DeLanyea wives that there would be no wedding feast tomorrow.

Trystan stood by the window, looking out at the night sky. Dylan couldn't be sure he was even listening.

"You and her Norman relatives needed proof that she was not a fit wife for you," Dylan continued.

Trystan's gaze remained on the view from his window. "How did you find out about Ivor?"

"Angharad."

"Ah."

"She told me when they would be together, and I devised the rest."

"Clever of you, that was."

"I didn't want to humiliate you, Trystan, but Norman witnesses were necessary."

"She's right, you know. It isn't fair that a man can dally with so few consequences, but a woman cannot."

"She's so proud of her Norman blood, she should not complain if she has to abide by Norman rules of conduct."

"I suppose not."

"Definitely not. So you'll go to Mair tomorrow?"

Trystan glanced at his cousin over his shoulder, his face shadowed. "Why would I go to Mair?"

"To ask her to be your wife, you nit. She's deep in love with you."

"No, she's not."

"You must be blind, or a fool if you believe that."

"I'm neither." Trystan turned and leaned wearily back against the sill. "She told me herself she doesn't love me enough to marry me."

"She loves you so much she can't bear to keep living here."

Trystan's brow furrowed as he crossed his arms. "What do you mean?"

"I mean, dolt, she's that heartbroken over losing you, she's running away. *Anwyl,* I never thought I'd see Mair surrender, but she'll do it for you."

"She wouldn't do that for me," Trystan replied gravely, moving away from the window. "And I'm sure she has another explanation."

"She *claims* she wants to be near Arthur."

"Mair doesn't lie."

"I've never known her to, but that doesn't mean she wouldn't if she thought she had to. God's wounds, Trys, can't you see? She never felt a need to leave Craig Fawr when our liaison was over, nor after any other."

"She's going to be with Arthur, like she said," Trystan insisted.

Dylan rose and approached his cousin, his expression as grave as Trystan had ever seen it. "I am going to admit something to you in great confidence, Trystan, because it embarrasses me to say this, even to you. I know now I was the consolation prize. She really wanted you all along."

Trystan's eyes narrowed with suspicious disbelief. "Then why didn't she tell me?"

"When she thought you didn't care for her? Can you see any woman of pride and spirit doing that? Mair would sooner cut out her tongue!"

"But after we...were together... She might have told me then."

"You *are* a nit—as well as the most ambitious DeLanyea since my own late, unlamented father. Do you think a woman who loved you would agree to marry you if she thought she would impede your progress to the rewards she believes you deserve?"

"I can't...I won't believe it."

"You had better, because it's the truth," Dylan affirmed. Then he started to laugh. "*Anwyl,* she might not think you the most wonderful man on earth if she could see you now, boy, looking as stunned as if you discovered snow was supposed to be red. The truth is as plain as the mole on Lady Rosamunde's breast, if you think about it."

He stopped smiling and regarded his younger cousin sympathetically. "She loves you so much, she tried to act as if she does not, for your sake."

Then he grinned his irrepressible grin as he strolled to the window and looked at the full moon. "She couldn't fool a man of my experience, of course. I don't know what it is about us DeLanyeas, but we never seem to really understand how a woman feels about us until it looks hopeless. Must be modesty, eh, Trystan?" He glanced back over his shoulder. "Trystan?"

But Trystan had already run from the room as if the castle were aflame.

Grinning broadly, Dylan strolled to the door. "I had better tell Lady Roanna she might be having a wedding feast tomorrow, after all."

"Wake up, Mair!" Trystan pleaded as he shook her gently.

She rolled onto her back and peered up at his face. It seemed to glow in the moonlight that streamed in through the open window and illuminated his anxious expression.

"What's the matter?" she demanded anxiously as she sat up, thinking the castle must be under attack or somebody dead for Trystan to come and rouse her on the night before his wedding.

The night before his wedding.

"Nothing's the matter—or everything," he said softly, "if you will still say you do not love me."

Dumbfounded, she stared at him incredulously. "Are you drunk?"

He smiled wistfully, and lovingly as he took her hands to pull her out of bed. The cold of the ground was a shock to her, yet nothing compared to the shock of his presence and the words he was saying.

"I assure you, Mair," he solemnly declared, "I have never been more sober. I love you! I need you! I want to marry you! Please say you will have me, fool that I am for not knowing my own heart sooner."

Scarcely believing her own ears or even the evidence of her eyes, she grabbed her blanket and wrapped it about her shoulders. "Sssh! You'll wake Arthur."

"I don't care if I do. I don't care if I wake the whole castle, or village, or all of Wales itself, if you tell me you love me."

She hastily found her shoes, then pulled him toward the door. "I never told you I loved you," she whispered, convinced he was drunk.

"To the brewery?"

"Yes," she hissed, "to the brewery, and keep your voice down, or you will cause a scandal!"

She pulled him outside and across her yard to the small stone building, thankful the moon was bright and there were no clouds to cover it. Otherwise, in her present confused state and his apparently deranged one, who could say what accident might befall them?

"There is already a terrible scandal in the castle," Trystan announced as he pushed open the door to the brewery, then gallantly gestured for her to precede him.

"What scandal? That the bridegroom has gotten completely drunk and is making enough noise to wake the dead?" she demanded as she struck flint and steel to light a rush and set it in a holder before facing him.

"No. That the bride has been found in bed with the captain of the guard."

Mair's jaw dropped as her eyes widened. "Ivor? And Rosamunde?"

"Exactly. Or Rosamunde and Ivor. Either way, they were making love and we caught them in the act, her fine, insolent cousin, the rest of the Norman wedding guests, Dylan, my father, my brother and me. After that, there is no question of a marriage between us."

"No question of a marriage?" Mair murmured, still not able to take in all that he was saying, and with such obvious glee.

"Yes. How could I wed her after the humiliation? What Norman would expect me to accept so dishonored a woman? Not a one! I confess it took me some time to realize that I should be thankful for Dylan and Angharad's interference—"

"Dylan and Angharad?"

Laughing, Trystan caught her by the hands and spun her around. "I fear something is amiss with your delightful ears, my love, my life."

He came to a halt and pulled her into his strong embrace, his expression suddenly serious. "I hope you can forgive my stupidity, Mair, for putting my ambition above everything else, even you. For trying to deny the feelings I have for you. For not seeing that without you, I could never be happy."

"But Rosamunde—?"

"Was a prize to prove I was better than my brother and my cousin, and only that, I came to see—not a woman I loved. I could never have loved her as I love you. As I have always loved you."

"You have always loved me?"

"Aye, although I tried to subdue it with passionate yearnings for women who were as unlike you as it was possible to be. Dylan's wife, at first, and then Rosamunde."

"You did a very good job, I must say. I certainly believed you loved them."

"Too good, for I was able to fool myself much of the time. God's wounds, if you hadn't grabbed me that night, I might have gone on fooling myself and been miserable because of it."

Her expression was still worried. "I know you

enjoyed making love to me, and I you, but making love is not the same as loving enough to marry.''

His face fell. "I know that. Are you saying you really do not love me enough to marry me?''

His grip on her hands tightened as his gaze grew more intense. "The truth, Mair,'' he begged.

She didn't meet his gaze. "You should marry a highborn lady, Trystan, who can help you in your quest, not an alewife who will make you the laughingstock of the Normans.''

"I do not want to marry a highborn lady. I want to marry you.''

"An alewife.''

"Yes, an alewife—a fine, bold, honest alewife, who smiles and laughs and makes me feel that life is a wonderful gift when I am with her.''

"But I cannot help you achieve what you should. I will…I will impede you.''

He drew back as if mightily offended. "Do you doubt my ability to succeed without the assistance of a wife's money or connections?''

"I know you can succeed with or without a wife's assistance. It is a wife's hindrance of which I speak.''

He smiled tenderly. "The greatest hindrance I could ever face would be to lose you, Mair. I know that now. Please say you will marry me, and then together we will see how far we can go.''

Her intense gaze searched his face. "Are you certain, Trystan? What will your parents say?"

His eyes shone. "I give you my word as a knight and a DeLanyea, I have never been more certain of anything than I am that they will give us their blessing. They like you very much. Indeed, I think my father would give his approval in an instant."

Her glorious smile thrilled him as joy filled her. "Then I must confess I love you, Trystan. For years I have done so."

"And hidden it as well, or better, than I hid my feelings," he noted, grinning as he pulled her into his arms again.

"Better," she said ruefully. "And since we are making confessions, I will admit I behaved with such anger after I first heard of Angharad's prediction about us because I feared somebody had guessed my secret, despite all my efforts."

"Indeed, I was convinced the very notion nauseated you."

"I thought the idea horrified you."

Trystan sighed and shook his head. "I should have realized sooner that your response wouldn't have upset me so much if I didn't really want you to like me."

"*Anwyl,* with the way I teased you, you *should* have hated me."

"Mair, that was the past. Will you make a new

beginning with me?" he pleaded softly. "Will you marry me?"

"Trystan...?"

"Say you will, Mair, and then kiss me, or I shall die."

"Oh, Trystan," she whispered through happy tears as he bent down to kiss her tenderly.

As her blanket slipped to the floor, his lips left hers to wend their way along her cheek. "Yes, Trystan," she murmured. "Yes, I will. Please God, I will!"

Then his mouth covered hers in a more torrid kiss and she surrendered herself to him, giving herself up to her joy.

"Do you know you taste better than *braggot?*" he whispered as he ran his hands through her thick, unbound hair.

"Do you know you smell better than honey?"

"Do you know you are the boldest, prettiest woman in Wales?"

"Do you know you are the finest man?"

The questions ceased as their lips met again.

"Mam?"

They both sprang apart to stare in surprise at a sleepy Arthur standing in the door, rubbing his eyes and peering at them. "What's *he* doing here?"

Chapter Fifteen

"Arthur, please go back to bed," Mair said.

She tried to maintain some parental dignity as she hastily retrieved the blanket and wrapped it around herself, but it was too late. Arthur was wide awake now.

"What's Trystan doing in the brewery?" he demanded. "Mam, why are you wearing a blanket?"

Looking slightly less confident than he had moments ago, Trystan took hold of Mair's hand.

"I am here to correct a terrible mistake. I am not going to marry Lady Rosamunde tomorrow," he started to explain.

"Oh," Arthur said as he nodded knowingly. "You've come to get drunk, then."

"He did not," Mair declared. "And where did you get such an idea?"

Arthur flushed and rubbed his toe on the floor.

"Some of the soldiers were talking one time, that's all."

"Perhaps I will have to keep you out of the castle, if you're going to eavesdrop and hear things you shouldn't," his mother warned.

A sulky expression clouded Arthur's face for an instant before he straightened his shoulders as defiantly as his mother might. "So why'd he come to the brewery, then?"

"I think you must be forgetting who you're talking to, Arthur," Trystan said before Mair replied "That's no way to speak to your mother, and the woman I have just asked to be my wife."

Arthur's mouth fell open.

"I love her very much, Arthur."

"And I love Trystan," Mair added, glancing up at him with a tenderness that belied the passion burning within her.

"As her nearest male relative, I hope you will make no objections," Trystan asked gravely.

Arthur regarded him studiously, then shook his head. "Anybody's better than that Ivor."

"Arthur!"

"He speaks his mind like his mother," Trystan said with a grin. "Or like his mother does *most* of the time," he amended.

"What happened to Lady Rosamunde?"

"Sometimes even when a man is grown, he doesn't know himself as well as he should," Trystan said, going to the boy and crouching down to see eye-to-eye with him. "And sometimes he tries to deny his own feelings because of something he thinks he needs."

Arthur's brow furrowed with confusion.

Trystan tried again. "Because of foolish ambition, I convinced myself I wanted Lady Rosamunde, when I really loved your mother all along."

Arthur looked past Trystan to his mother. "What does my da say?"

"Your da approves," Trystan replied.

Arthur nodded, then he grinned, and Mair seemed to breathe again. "Come, my son, let me take you back to the house."

"Let *us*," Trystan corrected, rising. He took Arthur's hand, then Mair's.

As they walked across the yard illuminated by the rushlight Mair carried, Arthur said, "Does this mean we have to live at Craig Fawr?"

"Not if you don't want to."

"When?"

"When will we marry? As soon as possible, I am thinking." He looked at Mair quizzically over her son's head.

"Aye, as soon as possible," she confirmed.

They reached the house. "To bed with you now, Arthur," Mair ordered.

Her son let go of their hands and went to the

ladder to the loft as Trystan put his arm around Mair's shoulder, delighting in the feel of her in his sheltering embrace.

Arthur started to go up, then paused and looked back, a worried expression on his young face. "You will be married before the baby comes?"

"Yes," Trystan said.

"Then the baby won't be—"

"No. He will be legitimate," Mair replied quietly, hoping her son would not be upset at the difference in the legality of his birth compared to his half brother.

Arthur shook his head sadly. "Poor thing," he murmured mournfully as he disappeared into the shadows.

Mair would have laughed aloud, had Trystan not stifled her merriment with a passionate kiss.

"I have never been happier, Mair," he sighed.

"Nor I. But you had best go back to the castle."

"Why?" he murmured, pressing light kisses along her neck.

"Because they will be wondering where you are."

"Dylan is so clever, he will surely guess."

"Arthur is awake."

"No, I'm not!" the boy called out.

"Arthur, go you to sleep at once." She gave Trystan a pointed look. "You see?"

She ran her hands up his broad chest. "Much as I would like you to stay," she whispered huskily.

"I don't want to go," he muttered, returning her caresses.

"Soon enough, I won't be wanting to let you out of my sight, or my hands," she said slyly, touching him intimately. "*Anwyl,* I will be attacking you any and every place beginning, I think, with the wall walk."

"Again? Is that a promise?"

Her throaty laugh dissolved into a sigh. "A vow, sir knight, and one I assure you I am very determined to keep."

"Then I had better warn the sentries…"

Early the next morning, after a night spent kissing and cuddling and nothing more because of their belief that Arthur might be awake, they sent Mair's obviously tired, yet elated, son to tell his half brother and Angharad the news.

It could not be denied that neither one of them particularly relished seeing her expression when she discovered her apparently faulty prediction was going to come true, after all.

After they had eaten a small breakfast, Mair and Trystan walked arm-in-arm toward Craig Fawr. Those in the village around the castle who were already stirring looked at them curiously; however,

Mair and Trystan were too engrossed in each other to pay much heed to anybody but themselves.

Suddenly Trystan halted and tugged her backward in the shadows of an alley between two thatched cottages near the main road leading to the castle.

"What are you doing?" she asked with a throaty chuckle.

Taking her in his arms, he smiled down at her. "Not that, Mair," he said with a low laugh and a lusty sigh, "tempting though it may be. I don't want Rosamunde to see us."

He nodded at the castle gates, and sure enough, Sir Edward D'Heureux and his daughter were making a hasty exit. Sir Edward looked like a defeated peasant; Rosamunde held her haughty head high.

Trystan and Mair remained in the shadows as the Normans, with their entourage, rode by.

"I can forgive her for loving Ivor because it broke the marriage agreement," Mair said, "but I cannot forgive her for accusing him of rape."

"No, nor I," Trystan agreed.

"A pity it is that Ivor must go. I don't think he would have gone behind your back and loved her if she had not encouraged him."

"Again, I agree—but he did make a serious mistake, for she was already betrothed. He betrayed our trust. If my father permitted him to stay, others might take it as a sign of weakness, and that he cannot permit.''

''How anybody could ever think you DeLanyeas weak is beyond me.''

''If they knew how we acted when we are in love, they might even think we are fools.''

''You are just men, that's all,'' she said sympathetically.

''What is that supposed to mean?''

She nestled against him. ''I'm not going to explain.'' She tilted her head to give him a mischievous glance. ''Ask Angharad.''

''Oh, no!'' Trystan cried in mock horror. ''I'm not asking Angharad anything, and I hope she doesn't tell me anything. I don't want to know the future beyond what I can guess—that I shall be blissfully happy with my shrew of a wife.''

''Shrew?'' Mair cried, shoving him away.

Trystan grinned. ''Disrespectful?'' He reached out and tugged her back as his voice lowered to a seductive murmur. ''Bold? Determined? Independent? Wonderful?''

Somebody cleared their throat very loudly, making them stop kissing and jump apart.

''*Anwyl,* what kind of immoral behavior is this?'' Dylan demanded sternly, his eyes dancing with merriment. ''Have you no bed to go to?''

''It's morning,'' Mair replied pertly. Her eyes

narrowed with amused suspicion. "What are you doing up and about so early?"

"I wanted to bid farewell to the beauteous Lady Rosamunde, and to make quite sure she hadn't run off with the silver. Then I got to wondering where Trystan had gone last night, so—"

"You knew full well," Trystan growled, his tone annoyed but he was unable to disguise the deep happiness that shone in his eyes.

"I suspected," Dylan corrected genially. "And not wrong, was I? You'd better get back to the castle, boy. Your da is waiting for you."

"How many times am I going to have to tell you to stop calling me 'boy'?"

"Maybe when you're married." Dylan's lips turned up in a devilish grin. "Boy."

"That's it!" Trystan cried as he moved Mair aside. He crouched and put up his fists, moving out of the alley toward his cousin. "Defend yourself, Dylan, while I show you how much of a man I am."

"Oh, don't be a nit!" Dylan said. "Only teasing, me, and—"

He barely avoided Trystan's fist, then dropped into a defensive crouch himself. "*Anwyl,* you're serious!"

"Absolutely."

"I think you're both acting like children," Mair

declared, her hands on her hips and an indulgent smile on her face.

"And this is the thanks I get for getting you out of that Norman wench's clutches?" Dylan demanded.

"This is what you get for a lifetime of teasing."

"Mair teased you more."

"I'm not going to marry *you*."

By now, a few of the villagers had come to see what was happening. When they saw the two DeLanyeas facing each other like wrestlers, they exchanged amused glances.

Until Trystan dived at Dylan, grabbing him around the legs and knocking him to the ground with a thud. Then the air filled with excited exclamations.

"You...you..." Dylan snarled as he struggled out of Trystan's grip.

"*Boy?* Has a *boy* knocked you down?" Trystan jeered as he again tackled his cousin.

"Da!" two young voices cried in unison.

Mair glanced over her shoulder and saw Trefor and Arthur running toward the combatants.

"It's all right, my sons," he said, panting, barely glancing at them as he kept his eye on his opponent. "A little fun we are having."

Trefor grinned. "You'll win, Da!"

"Thank you, my son."

"But why are they fighting? Is it because of

you?'' the more perceptive Arthur asked his mother as the men grabbed each other and fell to the ground, where they continued to wrestle and get muddier by the moment.

"Not at all," Mair replied as she tried to keep her eyes on the men who really were acting like children. She was tempted to get in between them and pull them apart.

On the other hand, Trystan had endured much from Dylan in the past, so perhaps it was better to let them fight and get the bad feelings exorcised like evil spirits.

"Your da has teased his brother for too long, and now look," she said, casting a surreptitious look at Trefor, for Trystan was definitely getting the better of his cousin.

As Dylan also realized, for he stopped trying to hit back, and cried, "I yield. God's wounds, I yield before you break my nose!"

"You are never going to call me 'boy' again, are you?" Trystan demanded triumphantly, his face filthy and his tunic torn.

"Very well. I won't call you 'boy' anymore," Dylan muttered.

Trystan climbed off his chest. "Good."

"I may start calling you worse," Dylan muttered as he rose with a grunt.

"You can't call him a bastard," Arthur noted gravely.

Dylan stared at his youngest son a moment, then burst out laughing. "*Anwyl,* no, I can't!"

He strolled toward the boys. "And Trystan was right to be angry. I have teased too much and now must pay the price."

He glanced down at his soiled, disheveled clothes. "Genevieve will have my hide for the damage to my clothes, but it's no more than I deserve. I'll have to make it up to her somehow," he said with a wink to Trystan and Mair.

Another group of horsemen came from the castle, this time with Sir Cecil at the head. As he and his cortege approached and passed them, he gave them a scornful look.

Trystan bowed with a flourish, followed quickly by Dylan.

"Farewell, Sir Cecil!" Trystan called out. "Good-bye to all your charming friends, too."

"And good riddance," Mair muttered beside him, causing everyone around to laugh with approval.

"Now, come you both to the castle," Dylan ordered as he straightened, "for the baron really is waiting for you."

Mair had been in the great hall of Craig Fawr too many times to count, yet never had she felt anything like the nervous tension she did as she entered this morning. In addition to the usual tenants and servants, the baron, his wife, Griffydd, his wife Seona, and Dylan's wife, the lovely Genevieve, were watching them approach.

Behind her and a very muddy Trystan came the equally muddy Dylan, one son on either side to escort him.

She should have worn her red silk gown, Mair thought anxiously, for once worrying about her attire.

Her blue wool gown was comfortable and neat and clean, but nothing like what a knight's wife should wear.

And she doubted she could ever act as a proper knight's wife should, either.

She felt Trystan squeeze her hand, and his reassuring grin comforted her. "Look you at my father," he whispered.

Mair did as he suggested and realized that Baron DeLanyea was trying very hard to look serious—unfortunately with little success.

Mair relaxed when she saw the welcome on his face.

Lady Roanna stood beside him, and as she smiled, Mair knew for certain everything was going to be well.

She was going to marry the man she loved, and they would not object.

She was so happy, her steps grew as light as if she were dancing.

"Good morning, Mair, Trystan, Dylan," the baron began, scrutinizing the group coming toward him.

"What have you boys been up to?" he asked, and he did not mean Arthur and Trefor.

"Your son picked a fight with me. That's gratitude, I must say," Dylan replied, not even trying to sound as if he were angry.

"It looks as if you had the worst of it," his wife noted, regarding him with some annoyance.

"Ah, now, Genevieve, he was angrier than I, so what chance did I have?" her husband said placatingly, giving her so charming a smile, she had no recourse but to forgive him, as she always did.

"And he won't call my husband-to-be a 'boy' anymore," Mair declared. She gave the baron a pert, mischievous smile. "And I don't think you should, either, my lord. I can well vouch for his maturity—and his virility, too."

"Mair!" Trystan warned as he crimsoned.

She carried on, irrepressible in her delight. "Baron, Angharad was right. I'm going to marry your son." She sighed with mock resignation. "It will pain me to have to ask her pardon for refusing to believe her before, but I am willing to make that sacrifice."

"Da," Trystan began in a reasonable tone.

He fell silent as his father hurried forward to take hold of Mair's shoulders and kiss her heartily on the cheek.

"God's wounds!" the baron cried happily, "a relief is this, and no mistake."

He looked to his son, and it would have been difficult to say whose smile was the more joyful. "Glad I am you came to your senses, my son! That Norman creature would have led you a dance."

"I will not argue that I have been too long realizing what I truly wanted." Trystan reached out to take Mair's hand. "What I needed."

His mother came forward in her own graceful way, and her shining eyes told Trystan that of all things he had done, this pleased her the most. "Welcome to our family, Mair. I know you will make my son happy, and he, you."

The other DeLanyea women hurried to offer their best wishes, then the other tenants and servants until Mair and Trystan were quite out of breath voicing their thanks.

"Roanna!" the baron called out above the commotion. "You had a wedding feast planned for today, did you not?"

"Yes, my love," she called back serenely from the other side of the large and noisy gathering.

"I see no reason not to have it today, after all."

"Nor do I, my love, nor do I."

And so it was that Sir Trystan DeLanyea wed Mair the alewife, who had teased him unmercifully and loved him since childhood.

And after their marriage, they loved so devotedly and so often that Arthur soon had four more half brothers, each one as notable a warrior as he came to be, and a sister who was famous not only for her beauty but, like her mother, for her vivacious, irrepressible spirit.

As for Trystan, he achieved all that he had ever wanted and more. He became famous throughout all the land for his wisdom and honor, so much so that no king's council was considered complete without him.

Or some of his wife's fine ale.

*   *   *   *   *

Mother's Day is Around the Corner...
Give the gift that celebrates Life and Love!

Show Mom you care by presenting her with a one-year subscription to:

For only **$4.96**—
That's **75% off the cover price.**

This easy-to-carry, compact magazine delivers 4 exciting romance stories by some of the very best romance authors in the world.

Plus each issue features personal moments with the authors, author biographies, a crossword puzzle and more...

A one-year subscription includes 6 issues full of love, romance and excitement to warm the heart.

To send a gift subscription, write the recipient's name and address on the coupon below, enclose a check for $4.96 and mail it today. In a few weeks, we will send you an acknowledgment letter and a special postcard so you can notify this lucky person that a fabulous gift is on the way!

This spring, make your destination The British Isles with four exciting stories from

Available March 2000

A WARRIOR'S KISS by **Margaret Moore**
(Wales)

and

THE VIRGIN SPRING by **Debra Lee Brown**
(Scottish Highlands)

Available April 2000

THE CONQUEROR by **Shari Anton**
Third book of
KNIGHTS OF THE BLACK ROSE
(England)

and

LADY OF THE KEEP by **Sharon Schulze**
(Ireland)

Harlequin Historicals
Where reading is truly a vacation!

Available at your favorite retail outlet.

◆ HARLEQUIN®
Makes any time special ™

Visit us at www.romance.net

HHMED11

She's stolen his heart, but should she be trusted?

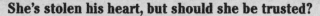

CANDACE CAMP

Lord Thorpe's new American business partner, Alexandra Ward, is beautiful, outspoken *and* the perfect image of a woman long thought dead. Her appearance on Thorpe's arm sends shock rippling through society, arouses hushed whispers in the night. Is she a schemer in search of a dead woman's fortune, or an innocent caught up in circumstances she doesn't understand?

Someone knows the truth, someone who doesn't want Alexandra to learn too much. Only Lord Thorpe can help her—if he can overcome his own suspicions. But even if he does, at what price?

A STOLEN HEART

*On sale mid-March 2000
wherever paperbacks are sold!*

MIRA

MCC552